BALANCING ACT

DIANE TUPPER

iUniverse, Inc.
Bloomington

Balancing Act

iUniverse books may be ordered through booksellers or by contacting:

iUniverse
1663 Liberty Drive
Bloomington, IN 47403
www.iuniverse.com
1-800-Authors (1-800-288-4677)

Because of the dynamic nature of the Internet, any web addresses or links contained in this book may have changed since publication and may no longer be valid. The views expressed in this work are solely those of the author and do not necessarily reflect the views of the publisher, and the publisher hereby disclaims any responsibility for them.

Any people depicted in stock imagery provided by Thinkstock are models, and such images are being used for illustrative purposes only.

Certain stock imagery © Thinkstock.

ISBN: 978-1-4697-5308-9 (sc)
ISBN: 978-1-4697-5310-2 (e)
ISBN: 978-1-4697-5309-6 (dj)

Library of Congress Control Number: 2012901430

Printed in the United States of America

iUniverse rev. date: 4/20/2012

Dedication

For my five children: Bob, Dave, Don, Michelle, and Deborah, who supported my decision to return to school as a 42-year-old "mature" student. They made the necessary sacrifices without too many complaints and were there at the finish line to yell, "Way to go, Mom!"

A special thanks to my daughter-in-law Lisa McDougall and my dear friend Sue McEvoy for their contributions in formatting and doing all the computer-related jobs that are beyond a Luddite like me.

Illustrations

The illustrations at the beginning of each chapter are the work of 11-year-old Sean Whiteside, one of the author's 13 grandchildren.

Chapter One

September
Peters v. Peters

Anxious not to be late for my first day as an articling student, I arrived at the front door of the law firm of McWilliams Cameron at 7:30 a.m., before anyone else and without a key or an umbrella.

In the hour I waited for someone else to arrive, I had plenty of time to reflect on the year on which I was about to embark.

Articling is the year you spend after graduating from law school during which you are a lawyer in training; it is the year that will determine whether or not you will become a "real" lawyer. It is a year in which you work at least 12-hour days, study at night for the bar exams, and, in my case, hope that you have some time and energy left for your children.

Hoping I would make it through the upcoming year, the last remnant of the feudal system, I tried to look like I had a reason to be hanging out on the street corner. It had just recently been vacated by Amanda, who, I subsequently learned, was 20 years younger than I, had a grade-nine education, and made about four times as much money in her chosen profession as I would make that year in mine.

This I learned on my second day on the job, after I had been given a key and been advised that I was expected to start work most days by 6:30 a.m., the time that Amanda was usually heading home.

Once Amanda realized that I was not trying to take over her corner, a supposition I found strangely flattering, she and I would occasionally vent our frustrations concerning our respective professions and clientele.

After I'd been standing on the corner for about an hour, getting progressively wetter, John McWilliams, the senior partner, finally arrived and ushered me into the building where I would begin my year of articles, without doubt the longest, most nerve-racking year of my life.

As soon as we were inside the building, John, who I later learned was manic-depressive and who was clearly in a manic stage, greeted me by shouting out that I must be the new "baby lawyer!" As I had graduated from law school at age 43 and was a single mother of three children, I was both taken aback and flattered to be called any name that sounded youthful rather than old; I was euphemistically known as the most "mature" student in my class.

John then proceeded to give me his version of an orientation, during which he dashed around the office moving files for no apparent reason and, at one point, threw all of his telephone messages in the garbage, explaining that they were so old there was no reason to return the calls. Over the next few days, I learned that John seldom returned calls but rather ignored them despite his secretary's pleas. It soon became one of my jobs to return his calls, and I was put in the position of trying to soothe irate clients and assure them that their case, about which in some instances I knew little or nothing, was going well.

Within 10 minutes of entering the office, I learned that it was being renovated and that there was not an office, a secretary, or even a desk for me. According to John, everyone who worked for him, including the renovators, was incompetent. He informed me immediately after this speech that I was to go to court in about one hour to get something called "short leave" on the Peters file. This was the sum total of my orientation.

When I spoke to some of my fellow articling students in the coming weeks, I discovered that they had had orientation weeks in which they were slowly and methodically introduced to the practice of law. They were given tours of their offices and the courthouse and introduced to the personnel in their firms and had the opportunity to observe client interviews and court cases. No one I spoke to was sent off to court the first day of his or her articling year, and many never went to court on their own all year.

After my "orientation," John dashed off, leaving me in the reception area. He reappeared in a few minutes and presented me with three boxes, which contained the Peters file. He then started up the stairs to his office shouting over his shoulder that I was to get short leave for an application for Mr. Peters to have access to his children.

As I sat in the reception area surrounded by the Peters file, various members of the firm began to arrive, along with other individuals who were obviously the incompetent renovators. Only the receptionist acknowledged my presence; she advised me that I would have to move, as the reception area was for clients only.

Trying not to panic, I took stock of my situation: I was soaking wet and being stared down by an intimidating receptionist; I had three large boxes, no time to read the files, no office, no desk, no idea what short leave was, and only a vague idea where the courthouse was located. Clearly, I needed help.

Out of sheer necessity, I somehow found the courage to approach the receptionist, who grudgingly pointed out John's secretary, Caroline.

Carrying two boxes, wishing as I would do many times in that year that I had taken a weight-lifting course, and assuring the receptionist I would be back for the third box, I made my way to Caroline's desk, which was already piled high with files, all of which were covered with a coating of drywall dust courtesy of the renovators, who were working on the ceiling directly over her head.

Caroline was a lifesaver that day, as she would be on many other occasions. Once I had explained my orders from John, she calmly brushed the debris from her hair, found the documents I needed to take to court, and explained that a short leave application was an application to have a matter heard sooner than the rules of court allowed. To be successful, one had to persuade the judge that the matter was urgent.

In this case, Caroline advised me, Mr. Peters wanted to take his children to Disneyland and had, in fact, bought the plane tickets. Mrs. Peters, who was outraged that she had been replaced by a younger version of herself, was taking the position that Mr. Peters could never see the children, especially if Debbie, the new love of his life, was also going on the trip.

It occurred to me as Caroline was outlining the foregoing that perhaps I could bring an application for an order that my former husband, who very seldom saw our three children, be forced to have access. As the year progressed, I encountered a surprising number of women who did not want their children's father to have access to them, usually to get back at him for ending the marriage. This I never understood. How are you punishing someone by taking on the sole responsibility of raising your children? Although I loved my children dearly, there were a fair number of occasions when I would have considered giving them to a total stranger for a day or two.

As it turned out, the courthouse was only about two blocks from my new place of employment, so I bravely headed down the street with the portion of the Peters file that I thought I needed but had had no time to read.

By the time I arrived at the courthouse, I was thoroughly intimidated and very cold and wet, since I had left my soggy coat at the office. Finding the building was not difficult, as it took up a whole city block. Finding where to go once I got in there was another matter. I wandered aimlessly for a few minutes, trying to appear as if I knew where I was going and what I was doing, but at five minutes to 10:00, the time I had been told that court began, I again realized that I needed help fast.

There was a sheriff standing outside one of the courtrooms, and I headed in his direction hoping that he would be able to save me from experiencing the shortest articling year on record. I dashed toward this poor young man, no doubt looking like one of the individuals that sheriffs occasionally had to escort from the courthouse. He looked genuinely frightened as I skidded to a stop in front of him. Fortunately, he did not reach for his gun.

Law school, I quickly realized, did nothing to prepare you for the real world of practising law. I had read hundreds of cases, argued and written exams on the principles and theory of law, and, with the rest of my class, been told by the Honourable Chief Justice in our law school orientation lecture, that I was the cream of the crop—one of the leaders of tomorrow.

As I stood in the courthouse begging the sheriff to save my skin, I felt a lot more like curdled milk than cream; I was a bedraggled 43-year-old straight-A student who had no clue how our judicial system actually worked.

The sheriff explained that there were lists posted showing in which courtroom a matter was to be heard and pointed me in the general direction of the lists. Trying to read the lists and find "Peters" was somewhat of a challenge, as they were taped to the wall and surrounded by a number of lawyers and lay litigants, all of whom were taller than my five-foot-one vertically challenged self.

After jumping up and down a few times, I was unable to spot "Peters" on the lists. Desperate, I asked one of the young lawyers who was blocking my view where short leave applications were heard. He informed me that I should go to courtroom 42, and, in his best condescending manner, stated that my case would not be on the list because, as it was a short leave request, no one knew I was coming. He then added, in case I was the complete idiot I appeared to be, that courtroom 42 was on the fourth floor.

I located the elevator, went up to the fourth floor, found courtroom 42, ran in, and proceeded to drop the Peters file, scattering the contents in various directions. What seemed like 100 pairs of eyes, including the judge's, all peered in my direction as I scrambled to pick up my documents, some of which had slid under the benches.

After a period of dead silence, the proceedings resumed, and I took a seat and tried desperately to put the papers back in the order that Caroline had so carefully arranged for me—a hopeless task, as I had no idea what sort of order I was trying to achieve.

I then sat for the next two hours while one lawyer after another was called to the front of the courtroom by the court clerk to make his or her arguments in support of various applications. I badly needed to use the washroom, wherever that was, but was afraid to leave for fear my case would be called in my absence. By about twelve o'clock, I was the only person, save for the judge, the sheriff, and the court clerk, left in the courtroom and still the Peters matter had not been called.

What I did not remember was that short leave applications were never on the list. What I learned was that one was supposed to advise the court clerk, before court began, that one had such an application.

At this point the court clerk said something to the effect of, "All rise; this court is no longer in session." In a panic, I stumbled to the front of the courtroom and announced to no one in particular, as I had no idea to whom I should impart this information, that I had an application for short leave.

The judge, who was halfway out the door, returned to his seat and asked me to state my name and tell him what my application was about. I did not have too much trouble with my name but did have trouble with his. Should I call him Your Honour, My Lord, Your Lordship? I settled for avoiding calling him anything.

I managed to explain my application by simply reading the affidavit that outlined the client's Disneyland plans and his ex-wife's refusal to hand over the children. His Honour, with thinly disguised amusement, said I could have my order and that it must be served on Mrs. Peters by 3:00 p.m. He then promptly left the courtroom.

In my supreme ignorance, I continued to stand at the front of the courtroom waiting for someone to give me a written version of the order. After asking why I was still there, the court clerk, who clearly wanted to lock up the courtroom, in what can only be described as a lofty sneer, advised me that it was my job to write up the order for the judge's signature. He further advised that I should have brought a draft of the order with me to court so that the judge could sign it.

With mixed emotions and as much dignity as I could muster, I left the courtroom. I had completed my first trip to court and obtained my order, but the whole ordeal had left me feeling as if I had just put in a 12-hour day, and it was only 12:30 p.m. I still had to get someone to type up the order, find the judge so he could sign it, and serve Mrs. Peters by 3:00 p.m.

When I returned to the office, it seemed that everyone had gone to lunch, except for the receptionist, who was clearly unlikely to be of any assistance, and a young man sitting in the reception area doing the *New York Times* crossword puzzle.

At first I assumed he was a client, as I did not think that anyone would be brave enough to disobey the receptionist's edict that the area was for clients only. However, as I entered the office, still wet and dishevelled, this fellow stood up and introduced himself as Patrick Cunningham. When I explained who I was and made a move to shake his hand, he backed away, probably afraid that I would drip on his impeccable outfit.

I soon learned that the receptionist, whose name, according to her prominently displayed name plate, was Jazmin, favoured Patrick, a 30-year-old associate lawyer. He was allowed to do many things that the rest of the firm, including the partners, were not. He regularly sat in her waiting room, used her telephone, and helped himself to supplies and the candy that she kept at her desk.

The rest of the staff were clearly afraid of her, as were the renovators, who were soundly chastised if they did not wipe their feet prior to entering the building and simply ignored if they had the nerve to ask to use her telephone.

I never learned how or why Jazmin had become so powerful, but, like everyone else, I tiptoed around her and simply avoided her as much as possible. This was not particularly easy as she was the keeper of all office supplies and the overseer of the office's only fax machine.

As it was already 1:00 p.m., I again needed help if I was to get my order typed and signed by the judge, whose name I had not thought to ask, and then serve it on Mrs. Peters, whose address was presumably somewhere in the three boxes of files.

It was unlikely that Jazmin would even acknowledge me, never mind help me. My only alternative was Patrick, who appeared only slightly more approachable than Jazmin. As I launched into the details of my predicament, Patrick sat impassively with his pen in hand, obviously anxious to get back to his crossword but too well brought up to ignore me completely.

Patrick, I subsequently learned, came from a very privileged background and had attended all the right schools. He went straight from high school to university and then to law school. Prior to practising law, he had never worked a day in his life. He was extremely literal and had no practical sense and limited people skills—which were very important in a law firm that practised almost exclusively family law.

The term *family law* is an odd designation, as all the clients we dealt with were breaking up or in the process of breaking up their families. They were also, in most cases, going through a very traumatic event in their lives; they were often distraught and unreasonable and badly needed to work with a lawyer who was skilled in dealing with their emotions as well as their legal problems.

When I approached Patrick this first day and outlined my situation, he stared at me blankly, as if to indicate that he did not see how any problem of mine could possibly have anything to do with him. His only response was to point out that John McWilliams was my principal and that I should speak to him.

Of course, John was nowhere to be found, as he was enjoying one of his typically—as I soon learned—extended lunch breaks. Many days, John simply did not return from lunch. I quickly realized that he could usually be located in a bar down the street. If he had not consumed too many beers, he was always willing to give me advice; in fact, when he was sober, he was an excellent if somewhat erratic teacher.

Although I did know how to type, having been a bookkeeper in my life before law school, I did not know how to use a computer; nor did I know the form on which to type up an order. Patrick, after filling in a few more answers in his crossword puzzle—in ink of course—finally volunteered that I could find sample orders in a precedent book, which was, unfortunately, located behind Jazmin's desk.

Out of sheer necessity, I approached the receptionist, introduced myself, and asked her if I could borrow the precedent book. Completely absorbed with the task of applying what looked like her ninth or tenth layer of nail polish, the iron lady failed to respond to or even acknowledge my presence in any way. Having no other options, I bravely repeated my request in a voice that I thought had the ring of authority.

Jazmin then very slowly screwed the cap back on her nail polish, blew on her nails for what seemed an unnecessary period of time, and then handed over the book, which was about a foot and a half thick and was extremely heavy. The advantages of a weight-lifting course again crossed my mind.

As I was staggering over to the table in the waiting room, carrying the book, my purse, and part of the Peters file, a fair load for anyone, never mind my 110-pound self, Jazmin again advised me that the waiting room was for clients only (and apparently Patrick). By now, it was about 1:30 p.m., and my fear of Jazmin was overshadowed by my fear of not getting my order typed, signed, and served by 3:00 p.m.

On the verge of tears, I told her that I had nowhere else to go, having no office and no desk, and that there were presently no clients in the waiting area. With this burst of assertiveness, I defiantly sat down on one of the "client" chairs and started madly looking through the enormous precedent book for a sample order. This was no easy task, as there was no index, many of the pages were loose, and the contents were in no apparent order.

Just as I had come to the conclusion that I should go back to being a bookkeeper, a job that had bored me to death but that I had at least understood and that had provided me with a desk, Caroline walked in the door. Hailing her, as I imagine one who was shipwrecked would hail a passing ship, I blurted out my situation. Caroline calmly removed her coat, patted me on the back, and guided me to her desk, advising that it would only take her a few minutes to type the order. As we were heading toward Caroline's desk, Jazmin, in her drill-sergeant-like voice, ordered us to return the precedent book, which I had left in the waiting room. We both simply ignored her.

True to her word, Caroline not only typed the order in just a few minutes but also telephoned the courthouse and obtained the name of the judge, His Honour, Judge Bartlet, who had heard my application.

The next step was to run to the courthouse and find the judge so that he could sign my order. It was now almost 2:00 p.m., and the order had to be served on Mrs. Peters by 3:00 p.m. Caroline did suggest that next time—if I survived the day—I should ask for more time to serve the order but also reassured me that we would get it served on time as long as I could quickly locate Judge Bartlet.

As I hobbled down the street to the courthouse in my new high heels, purchased especially for my first day on the job, I made a mental note to revert back to my less-fashionable but infinitely more comfortable flats.

Caroline had told me to go to the court registry, family division, and explain that I needed my order signed on an urgent basis. The court registry is located on the first floor, which is called the second floor and is one floor down if you enter the building at the south end but the floor on which you enter if you use the north entrance. The logistics added several minutes to my search and to my rising level of panic.

At about 2:15, I found the right counter, where, much to my relief, there was only one person in front of me. English was apparently this woman's second language, which prompted the clerk to do what many of us do when confronted with someone whose mastery of the English language is minimal; he talked very slowly in a very loud voice. Finally, after concluding that they were not communicating, the clerk indicated that he would get an interpreter, asked the lady to sit and wait, and then addressed himself to my problem.

Like Caroline, the clerk was efficient and helpful, except that he continued to talk loudly, as if I too was new to the English language. The effect of this was that everyone in our immediate area soon became aware that a 43-year-old "baby lawyer" had managed to get herself into a near-impossible situation. I now had about half an hour to get my order signed and served.

The clerk said he would try to locate the judge. He suggested that, meanwhile, I telephone my secretary and arrange for a process server to be at my office when I returned. Not having a secretary of my own, I telephoned the ever-calm and efficient Caroline, who, it turned out, had already made these arrangements.

At 2:45 p.m., I burst through the front door of the office clutching my signed order, half expecting Jazmin to scold me for running in the waiting room. If she did, I didn't hear her, as I was focused on Caroline and a fellow, presumably the process server, both of whom were doubled over with laughter. The source of their amusement was the photograph supplied by Mr. Peters for the purpose of identifying Mrs. Peters when she was served.

The picture was half of a torn photograph. In it, Mrs. Peters was standing in front of a heart background in her wedding dress. It struck me then, and has never failed to amaze and sadden me, how heartless people can be to the person they once promised to love until "death do us part."

Caroline had determined that Mrs. Peters was at work and calculated that if the process server hit all the green lights, she could be—and was—served by 3:00 p.m.

Just as Caroline and I were high-fiving each other and I was breathing almost normally for the first time that day, John McWilliams returned from his extended lunch and asked us what we were celebrating. Feeling rather proud of myself, I told him I had successfully obtained the short leave order and that Mrs. Peters had been served. I did feel somewhat deflated when John said that lawyers always got short leave orders, as if it was no big deal. Well, it was a huge deal for me, and I was determined not to let John's nonchalance spoil my high.

John started to head toward his office, which was on the building's second level. Meanwhile, I headed toward the washroom, which I had needed to use for a number of hours. Just as I opened the ladies' room door, John, who was halfway up the stairs, yelled that I was to follow him. My need for the washroom at that moment was greater than my inclination to obey John instantly. However, I was nervous enough to make my trip as quick as possible, which was probably a good thing, as an extended view of me in the mirror would not have been of benefit to my self-esteem.

After my brief trip to the washroom, I scurried up the stairs as fast as my new high heels would allow. Finding John's office was no problem, as he was on the telephone berating some poor client, who apparently had not followed his advice to hang up the phone when her estranged husband repeatedly called her. At the time, I thought that his tone was rather harsh, but, although my manner was somewhat softer, throughout the year, I was struck by how many clients, especially women, complained about repeated phone calls but failed simply to hang up.

John motioned for me to come in while he was still on the telephone. His office was stacked high with files—on his desk, on the chairs, on his credenza, and on the floor. I cleared a chair, took a seat, and looked around while he yelled at his client. The chaos was mind-boggling, but I came to learn that John knew where everything was and heaven help anyone who moved a file, including his secretary, who would wait until he was out and then very carefully do the filing or find a document she needed or a file for me that John had told me to handle.

After finally finishing his telephone diatribe, John muttered under his breath about "this damn stupid woman" and then launched into the first of many "lessons" he would give me over the year. I learned to listen carefully because, despite his often outrageous behaviour, John was an excellent teacher in his own way. One had to really listen as the lesson was often contained in his recounting of a case or his criticism of another lawyer.

At about 5:00 p.m., John remembered that he had a court application the next day and he needed me to get him case law on spousal support, which was impossible to do unless you knew the facts of the particular case, as there are thousands of cases dealing with spousal support. When I tried to pin him down to at least get the name of the file, he suggested we go to the local bar for a drink and he would give me the information I needed over a beer.

I had been in my high heels for almost 12 hours, so a drink sounded appealing, but only at home after I had checked in with my children. However, when the senior partner asks you to go for a drink, especially on your first day of work, you go for a drink. Besides, I needed some information about the next day's application so that I could attempt to find the pertinent law.

While John was "organising" his desk, I managed to step out into the hall and make a quick call home. My 16-year-old daughter, Sarah, who answered the telephone, sounded disappointed that it was only me and then let me know in no uncertain terms that Morgan and Mitchell, my 11-year-old twins, had not done their homework and had eaten a carton of ice cream instead of the healthy snacks that I had left for them. According to Sarah, they were presently playing a game in which you kept hitting the other person's arm to see who could cause the worst bruise.

Sarah had been a great help to me when I first returned to school, loading and unloading the dishwasher, vacuuming, washing clothes, and even starting dinner; however, as she hit her mid-teens, her focus was more on boys, clothes, and talking for hours on the telephone, and her helpfulness to me was somewhat diminished and unpredictable. The twins also had chores they were responsible for, but they usually spent more time arguing about whose turn it was than it would have taken just to finish the chore. In other words, they were, in my view, pretty normal kids.

I told Sarah I would try to be home in an hour and that I would pick up a pizza on the way home; it would be the first of many pizzas, I am sad to admit, that my children lived off that year. Sarah wanted to chat. Anyone who has had a 16-year-old girl knows that they do not always want to chat with their mothers, so you usually drop everything when you are acknowledged as a real person in whom they want to confide. Unfortunately, I had to end our telephone call as John was now standing beside me, motioning that I should follow him down the stairs.

This was only the first of many occasions on which I had to weigh what my boss wanted against what my children needed; it was a balancing act that I never felt I got right.

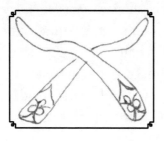

Chapter Two

October
Hrayzickiw v. Hrayzickiw

*I*somehow survived a whole month at McWilliams Cameron, despite several harrowing and sometimes embarrassing trips to court and the general chaos in the office, which was made worse by my lack of an office, secretary, desk, or even my own chair.

Instead of at my own desk, I worked in the boardroom if it was not being used, and if it was someone else's office while he or she was in court. Sometimes, I worked on the stairs, the walls of which were lined with shelves that contained reference books, and more than once, I sat on a pile of lumber which the incompetent renovators had not yet used. If none of the foregoing was available, I took work next door to the coffee shop and ordered cups of coffee I did not want, simply to have the use of a table for an hour here and there. Except at lunchtime, the coffee shop was not very busy, so no one seemed to mind my presence; in fact, I became quite friendly with one of the waitresses who, in exchange for a few juicy tidbits from my files, would let me occupy a table for a considerable length of time. The tidbits were, of course, made up, as even I knew enough not to mess with solicitor-client privilege.

Some of my September experiences were embarrassing; some were harrowing; some were scary; and many were just plain exhausting. Some days I hardly saw my children, and many days I felt that I was not measuring up as a mother or a lawyer.

John would often take a long lunch and then barrel into the office about 4:00 p.m. looking for the baby lawyer so that he could give me instructions as to what he needed me to do for his court application the next day. Often he needed me to research some point or area of law. Usually I had to scurry after him, trying to get the facts of the case and, in some instances, even the name of the file. Then I had to find the file, which was not an easy task, as it could be in John's office or in someone else's office, on his secretary's desk, or in the file room where files were stored in no particular order.

Once I had located the file and got at least a general idea about which law was required, I invariably had to organize the contents and find the necessary letters and documents, which were scattered around John's office, and then check in the "to be filed" area behind Caroline's desk. This was the easiest part of the process, because although Caroline was too busy to keep up with the filing, she did have an alphabetical file folder, which was usually in pretty good order, unless of course John had rifled through it before she could stop him.

Once I had found the cases that I thought were relevant, I had to make three copies of each case—one for John, one for the opposing counsel, and one for the judge. Inevitably, by the time I had found and copied the cases, everyone else would have gone home or to the neighbourhood bar. At this point, I still had to highlight the relevant paragraphs, as John very seldom read the whole case and simply depended on my highlighting, a practice that put unbelievable pressure on me. Then I had to bind the cases with a machine I never fully mastered and leave them on Caroline's desk so that she could complete a cover page and an index the next morning.

On the days when I was the last person in the office, my final task was to arm the security system. I had to set the alarm, run to the door, and lock it. Sometimes, it was 9:00 or 10:00 p.m. before I finally left the office. By then, it was dark and often raining as I made the dash to my car grasping my keys, my only weapon in case I was accosted in the parking lot. Our parking lot was between our office and a homeless shelter. I never was accosted, but twice in my first month of articling, I had to wake up a homeless person who had fallen asleep—or more likely passed out—behind my car.

One night, I was working in an upstairs office and did not realize that everyone else had gone home. Apparently, the last person to leave did not know that I was still in the office so he or she set the alarm. When I started down the stairs, it triggered the alarm. No one had told me how to turn the alarm off or the phone number of the alarm company. As I hunted for the off button, which I later found out was located under a secretary's desk, the alarm continued to blare for about 25 minutes until the alarm company phoned to see if there was a problem and subsequently turned off the alarm at their end. Understandably, I never had much faith in the alarm system after that in light of the length of time it took them to respond; added to that was the fact that if someone other than me was the last to leave, which was not often, he or she usually forgot to set the alarm at all. This meant that if I was the first to arrive in the morning, which I generally was, I invariably conducted a morning patrol of the office before I could comfortably get to work, if the alarm had not been set.

In about the last week of September, John decided that I was ready to go to court and speak to an uncontested divorce. I learned from Caroline that once a week, a courtroom was assigned for uncontested divorces and that lawyers one after another got up and asked their respective clients a series of questions, which took about as long as your standard wedding vows, after which the judge gave them the order for divorce or, in other words, pronounced that they were no longer man and wife. Of course, in his usual fashion, John decided I would do this about 45 minutes before court started.

Caroline gave me a printout of the questions I had to ask, and about 15 minutes later, John introduced me to the client, Ted Richardson. Shortly thereafter, Mr. Richardson and I walked to the courthouse, with me attempting to carry on a conversation while at the same time trying to remember the questions so that I would not have to read them. I figured that if I could ask the questions without referring to my "cheat sheet" too often, I could appear to be someone who did this all the time. It was surprisingly easy to "talk" to Mr. Richardson; all I had to do was nod every so often as he listed all the things that were wrong with his soon-to-be ex-wife.

I learned throughout the year that the majority of clients had absolutely nothing good to say about their spouse, a person whom they had in the past promised to love and cherish until one of them died. The person they were vilifying was someone they had chosen, so what did that say about them? Had all of these people made the choice to marry someone with no good qualities?

Mr. Richardson and I easily found the right courtroom as, after my first disastrous trip to court, I had gone to the courthouse on my own and familiarized myself with the layout. The courtroom was packed with lawyers and their clients. It was so full that I did not see John standing at the back of the courtroom. By then, I knew enough to identify myself to the court clerk before Mr. Richardson and I took a seat and waited for the judge to arrive and our case to be called.

As it turned out, my case was the second one, so the courtroom was still crowded. Mr. Richardson took the stand and was sworn in. I proceeded to ask the relevant questions. I was thankful it went quite smoothly. I was feeling pretty good about myself until, just as Mr. Richardson and I were about to leave the courtroom, John, to my overwhelming embarrassment, announced to the courtroom that I was his baby lawyer, that this was my first uncontested divorce, and that clearly he had taught me well. At least I think that is what he said, as my sole focus was on getting out of the courtroom as quickly as possible.

I was concerned that Mr. Richardson would say something about John's outburst, but he did not. In his self-absorption over his own situation, a common trait of people going through a divorce, on the way back to the office, he continued to list his now ex-wife's faults.

I returned to the office, and after sending Mr. Richardson on his way, I was confronted by the other partner in the firm, Ruth Cameron, better known as "Ruthless" Cameron. Confrontation was the manner in which Ruth dealt with everyone, including her partner John. Ruth, who was about to turn 60, was neurotic, often vague, and also demanding, That day, she demanded that I take over the Hrayzickiw file, as she no longer wished to deal with the client.

However, Ruth's way of giving me the file was to talk to me about it incessantly and to second-guess everything I did. After I had a chance to read the file, I thought that there was very little left to do. The parties, who were in their late sixties and fairly well off, had divided all of their assets, including the former matrimonial home, a summer cabin, and various investments and pensions. All that was left was the division of some household items and deciding who would end up with their cat.

Because of my inexperience, I did not realize that many people can deal with the big issues, but because they want to feel that they have "won," they do not want to end the connection, or, as many clients told me, "It was the principle of the matter." They continue to pay lawyers far more than the items they are fighting over are worth. In one case that I dealt with later in the year, the couple settled everything except who would get the VCR, an item worth about $200 at the time. The lawyer on the other side actually telephoned me to see if I would like to chip in for a VCR. Eventually, after both parties had spent considerably more than $200, they settled the matter by flipping a coin.

We acted for Mrs. Hrayzickiw, whose marriage had been what the courts refer to as a "traditional marriage." Mr. Hrayzickiw had run his own car parts company, and Mrs. Hrayzickiw had stayed at home and raised the couple's five children. Mr. Hrayzickiw gave his wife a cash allowance each week for household and personal items; he paid all the bills, looked after car maintenance and insurance, and looked after all of the household banking.

At 68 years old, Mrs. Hrayzickiw had never written a cheque or had a credit card. For 45 years, her job was to look after people. Now, her children were grown with families of their own, and she had been traded in for a younger model.

One of the mistakes I made with Mrs. Hrayzickiw was to give her my home phone number. This is a *big* mistake when you are dealing with family law clients. She phoned me at all hours—at night and on the weekends. Sometimes, it was just to talk, as she was terribly lonely. She often sounded drugged, which I subsequently found out she actually was. Her doctor was in the practice, as were a number of doctors whose patients, usually women, were going through a divorce, of prescribing sleeping pills, "wake up" pills, antidepressants, and so on, as it was easier to write a prescription than to find a positive way to help her. After one appointment, in which she was obviously drugged and sleepy, she left my office and backed her car into a pole in the parking lot next door.

Mrs. Hrayzickiw also telephoned me to ask how to do a number of things that her husband had always done, such as renew her car insurance, open a bank account, have her car serviced, and apply for a credit card. After Mrs. Hrayzickiw and other clients continued to phone me with matters they thought were urgent, I applied for an unlisted number. After all, there was nothing I could do for them in the very little time I had after work with my children and if something was really urgent, it was the police, not I, whom they should be calling.

The cat that the Hrayzickiws were fighting over was an expensive breeding stud. Who knew there was such a thing? Well, apparently, Ruth Cameron did, or so she said. Not wanting to do any of the legwork herself, Ruthless, who had three cats of her own and therefore saw herself as a cat expert, gave me the names of people who actually valued cats. She also managed to corner me on a number of occasions so that she could talk to me about the breeding process—information that I could have lived without.

Ruth also invited me to a cat show, on the pretext that I would gain information for our case. The invitation, which I did not know how to get out of, was really because she had no one else to go with. This was another evening away from my children and one I really resented, as I could not even justify it as work-related. It was also incredibly boring watching one cat after another being paraded around the ring with its proud owner, while Ruth kept up a running commentary about which cats she preferred and why.

Because there were only the issues of the cat and household items, the other lawyer and I decided that a settlement conference was a better choice than going to court where a judge would probably berate us (the lawyers) for wasting the court's time on such trivial matters. These matters were not, however, trivial to the Hrayzickiws.

It was agreed that the settlement conference, my first, would be held in our firm's boardroom. My client arrived first, about 45 minutes before the appointed time, so that we could go over, for about the fifth time, the list of the items she wanted, which included the souvenir spoons that the couple had collected during their various trips. Mrs. Hrayzickiws was very nervous and had applied too much makeup, somewhat pathetically, wanting to look good for her husband. She also seemed to be more drugged than usual.

I made a pot of rather strong coffee and took it, four mugs, and Mrs. Hrayzickiw into the boardroom. After I had poured her a cup, hoping the caffeine would counteract the drugs, I left her while I went downstairs to usher Mr. Hrayzickiw and his lawyer up to the boardroom. Unfortunately, we met John on the stairs. I had to make introductions, a task which made me nervous, as you never knew what John would say, and I had never mastered the pronunciation of the Hrayzickiws' last name. Fortunately, John was in a rush to get to court and did not make one of his "baby lawyer" remarks, nor did Mr. Hrayzickiw appear to notice my mangled pronunciation of his name.

The settlement conference was eventually productive but very sad and, in a twisted way, amusing. Mr. Hrayzickiw entered the room, wearing a thick gold chain, a common accessory for men going through their "midlife crisis" or in this case, "old-age crisis." What was left of his hair was dyed black and styled in a very odd comb-over. He avoided looking at his estranged wife, who was weeping quietly onto a pad of paper I had given her to make notes. I gave her the ever-present box of tissue and took my time pouring coffee, hoping Mrs. Hrayzickiw could pull herself together.

The issue of the cat was settled fairly quickly but not before an electrician, who had obviously been listening to our discussion, had poked his head through the partly finished ceiling and contributed his view that cats were useless creatures and that he was a dog person. Even Mrs. Hrayzickiw managed a smile at this bizarre interruption. After this, and perhaps because the electrician's appearance had lightened the mood, the parties agreed to joint custody of the cat. We then spent about an hour working out a rather complicated yearly schedule.

Who would get the souvenir spoons was more difficult and, from my point of view, hard to understand. Both parties wanted them, presumably so they could fondly remember the trips they had taken together before their marriage fell apart. There were about 30 spoons hanging from a wooden rack, which appeared to be one of those rather inexpensive ones people buy at souvenir shops. We finally decided that they would take turns picking the ones they wanted. We did this, but then there was the issue of who got the spoon rack, a rack that would now be only half full. Mrs. Hrayzickiw tearfully explained that she did not want Mr. Hrayzickiw to have it, and Mr. Hrayzickiw, perhaps with a twinge of guilt, finally agreed that she could have the spoon rack.

Mrs. Hrayzickiw left the office after I had explained the next step in her case, which involved me going to court and reading before a judge the terms of our cat/spoon consent order. I was not looking forward to this trip to court, which would surely evoke snickers from the other lawyers in the courtroom and, quite likely, from the judge. I felt extremely bad for this older woman, who was going to return to her empty house with spoons that could only be a sad reminder of the huge gap in her life. Although many nights I dreamed of returning to a quiet, empty house, that night, I actually felt very happy to return to a full, noisy, somewhat cluttered house, where I was needed.

Diane Tupper

Chapter Three

November
Nottingham v. Nottingham

Not having an office or a desk made working complicated, but it was manageable, as I became quite adroit at scouting out empty offices. And, after the first few weeks, one of the incompetent tradespeople took pity on me and fashioned a desk-like setup that looked rather odd but worked surprisingly well.

Not having my own secretary was a much bigger problem, particularly as secretaries, who, tired of drywall dust on their desks, files, and hair and workmen commenting on their appearance, left as soon as they could find another job. The only one who stuck it out was Caroline, who calmly went about her work, despite the chaos.

Caroline would do my work when she had time, which wasn't often. When she was not available, I worked at befriending the other secretaries. However, because of the turnover, I no sooner found someone who would do some of my work than that person would also leave for a less-stressful environment.

At first, it was surprising to me that clients would stay with the firm, even though they had to manoeuvre around hanging electrical wires, piles of lumber, and workmen in order to get to their lawyer's office. After I had been there a while, I realized that most clients were so wrapped up in their problems that they hardly saw their surroundings. Mrs. Nottingham was one of those clients. She lived and breathed the details of her case, details that were often not relevant but which she wanted to unload on someone. That someone quickly became me.

Mrs. Nottingham was Ruth Cameron's client, but Ruthless did not have the patience to deal with her, so I became her audience by default. I really didn't mind as it meant that I had the use of Ruth's office. Ruth would call me into her office when Mrs. Nottingham arrived and then make some excuse that she had to get something and simply never return.

I spent hours listening to Mrs. Nottingham, who was sure her husband was hiding assets, which I suspected he was. They owned a number of companies and investments as well as a very large house and a summer cottage. Mrs. Nottingham knew next to nothing about the companies and really just wanted her lifestyle to continue, which it would not.

Everyone wants a bigger piece of the settlement pie, but no matter how you slice it, both parties suffer financially in a divorce. Those who spend thousands of dollars on lawyers and who tell you they would rather spend their money on lawyers than settle with their spouse suffer more, and those who end up in a trial suffer the most.

Ruth's secretary at the time, Tara, basically ran Ruth's practice. She was very smart and extremely organized and managed to work in the mess that was Ruth's office. The chaos included a mass of plants, which, very quickly, it became my job to water. Ruth actually managed to work very little.

She was seldom in the office before 10:00 a.m. and spent a great deal of time simply wandering around and bothering people who were trying to work. She left everything to the last minute. On more than a few weekends, she advised me on Friday afternoon that an argument was due on Monday and I would have to come in on the weekend to help her. What this meant was that I worked all weekend with Ruth showing up late on Sunday to see what I had done. She would then spend the next week saying how tired she was after working all weekend.

At first I wondered how she kept her job and why John McWilliams put up with her. I later learned that she came from a very wealthy family and they owned the building in which the law firm was situated, which guaranteed her a job.

Mrs. Nottingham's case was a relatively complicated one and should not have been in the hands of an articling student. That being said, I certainly learned a lot from the case—with Tara's help. I learned who you called when you wanted a company or wine collection valued, which expert reports were necessary, and generally, how to get a file ready for trial.

I prayed that Tara would stick it out at least until the Nottingham case was either settled or went to trial. Gia, Tré and J. C., the Nottingham's poor children, were the subject of reports as to who should have custody. This involved many interviews with the children themselves, plus teachers, friends, and relatives. Both parties hired their own expert, so the children were put through the whole process twice.

Issues with respect to children seem to bring out the worst in some parents, especially those who feel it is appropriate to discuss the case with the children and to run down the other parent. I tried to explain to Mrs. Nottingham that she and Mr. Nottingham would have to deal with each other for the rest of their lives with respect to the children. There would be graduations, weddings, and probably grandchildren. She did not want to hear what I had to say. Her view was that they were her children and her husband should see them as little as possible because he was the one who wanted the divorce.

As I learned more about the Nottingham's life, I found out that Mr. Nottingham had been and wanted to continue to be an involved father. He coached many of the teams the children played on, went to parent-teacher meetings, took them camping, and was genuinely heartbroken that his wife had cut him off from the children.

Sadly, if one parent, usually the mother, wants to deny the other parent access, he or she is often successful. There are remedies at law, including finding the parent in contempt of court and sending him or her to jail. This is very seldom done as judges are reluctant to send the children's primary caregiver to jail.

A parent can also be fined for denying access, but again, judges are loath to put an added financial burden on the parent. If a parent is refusing to give the other party the access provided for in an order, there is a peace officer clause, which can be added to the order. However, this too is rarely used, as having a couple of police officers turn up at the house to get the children is a provision the access parent usually refuses because of the effect on the children.

If a parent continually refuses access, in a few cases, the courts have given the other parent custody. This too is rare. Some access parents simply give up, as the financial and emotional cost is simply too great.

At a four-way meeting that we set up to try to settle at least some issues, Mrs. Nottingham used the occasion to berate her husband for everything she could think of, while Mr. Nottingham just kept saying that he wanted to see his children. This was actually a five-way meeting, as Ruth knew very little about the case and needed me there to fill in the blanks.

Needless to say, nothing was settled, but I saw a man who just wanted to see his children and who was in tears by the end of the session. I hoped that Mrs. Nottingham would soften her position on access as she came to terms with the separation.

Mr. Nottingham's wish to see Gia, Tré and J. C. was in stark contrast to my own situation. My former husband took our three children out to lunch about once a month. He did not come to their games or their school functions, even though I faithfully sent him lists of their upcoming games and events. I did this for years, somehow hoping that he would change. He never did.

Because I was the only parent in my children's lives, I felt terribly guilty when I had to work late and on weekends. I had gone back to school to get my law degree so that I could better provide for my children financially, but set off against the higher wages was the lack of time I had to spend with them. The mental picture of the scales of justice with time balanced against money came to mind often as I struggled with my guilt.

My children never complained about my long hours. To be honest, I think they liked the freedom they enjoyed when I was not home. So far, none of them had abused that freedom in any major way, but I was cognisant of the pitfalls of the teen years.

Don't get me wrong; my children did get away with things that they would not have if I was home. For example, none of them made their bed, as they could not see the point when they were just going to mess it up the next night. I am also sure that they watched more TV and ate more junk food than they would have if I had been home.

The big issue was showers. My daughter took two to three a day, and the boys took as few as possible. One weekend, when it was clear that they had avoided showering to the point that they had an unpleasant smell, I actually pushed them both into the shower, clothes and all. Not my best parenting moment, but they did strip down and actually used soap and shampoo.

One of the family assets in the Nottingham case was a rather extensive and expensive wine collection, which only came to light some months after the parties' separation. Although Mrs. Nottingham had given me extensive lists of household items, including such things as six cleaning rags in the carport, and lists of all of the food that was in the house when she left it, she failed to mention the wine collection.

Mrs. Nottingham and the children had moved out of the family home to a large rental house, as Mrs. Nottingham could not bear to stay in the former matrimonial home. This left Mr. Nottingham in the seven-bedroom, 6,000-square-foot house all by himself. It also meant that he was maintaining two households, as Mrs. Nottingham did not work outside the home. It was a silly and expensive setup, but Mrs. Nottingham was a rather silly woman with no sense of the cost of maintaining two residences.

The wine collection was in the wine cellar in the former family home. When Mrs. Nottingham finally got around to mentioning it, I arranged for a wine appraiser to attend the home so that we could determine what it was worth. After arranging a suitable time through Mr. Nottingham's lawyer, the wine appraiser went to the house and found exactly three bottles of wine. Mr. Nottingham and his friends had apparently managed to drink the rest—about 200 bottles.

Now, whether Mr. Nottingham and his buddies actually drank the wine or he moved the collection to a storage facility, we will never know. His argument was that he was so distraught at not seeing his children that he drowned his sorrow in wine. As Mrs. Nottingham had no idea what wine her husband had collected, it was difficult to ascribe a value to the collection. When this matter finally went to trial, the judge gave it a value of $5,000. I saw Mr. Nottingham smile when the judge gave his ruling, making me think that the figure was substantially lower than the real value.

A few weeks after the wine incident, I was relating the story to another lawyer, who, without a doubt, had a better story, which showed how crazy people can be. His client was very upset that he was ordered to give his wife of only five years one-half of the value of his house. Rather than abiding by the order, he borrowed a bulldozer and bulldozed one-half of their home. The lawyer swore that this really happened but did not know the outcome as he fired his client, for obvious reasons.

My articling year was an eye-opener as to how unreasonable, fixated, childish, and really mean people can be when going through a divorce. I am sure that many of our clients were reasonable human beings until they were faced with the issues that arise out of a divorce. We definitely see them at their worst.

Another eye-opener was the lawyer meetings our firm held about once a month. There was always beer and pizza, which was a mistake. Poor Patrick, who was in charge of the meetings, would carefully type up an agenda and make copies for everyone. We would typically get through about two items before the beer kicked in and John's and Ruth's voices got louder and louder as they tried to outtalk each other.

The meetings became a free-for-all, with John and Ruth pointing out each other's faults. To give him credit, Patrick would keep trying to bring the meeting to order. This was a mistake, as

Ruth and John would both start yelling at him. The October meeting was particularly unruly, with John and Ruth actually throwing pizza at each other. Patrick gave up when a slice of pizza landed on his impeccable suit.

At this point, Patrick and I left the room and left the two partners to duke it out. In November, Patrick, relying on hope over experience, gave us all a neatly typed agenda. At that month's meeting, Patrick displayed the only humorous side of himself I ever saw when he arrived at the meeting with a full-length plastic apron. Only he and I saw the humour in it, as Ruth and John had obviously forgotten or seen nothing wrong with their behaviour during the October meeting.

The Nottingham trial was set, or so we thought, for the last week of November. Tara and I spent hours organizing the great stack of documents into three sets of books. On Ruth's request, I prepared her opening and closing statements, cross-examinations of Mr. Nottingham and his witnesses, and examination of our witnesses. I also put together the case law, which I thought we needed, and, with Tara's help, completed the books.

Ruth kept saying she was getting ready for the trial, but we saw no evidence that she was. I was starting to panic, as being an articling student, I could not do the trial, and I knew that Ruth had done virtually nothing to prepare.

The first day of the trial arrived, and Ruth and I and Mrs. Nottingham headed to the courthouse. On the way, Ruth started asking me basic questions like, "How old are the children?" and "What are their names?" Fortunately, Mrs. Nottingham did not overhear our conversation, as she cried all the way to the courthouse.

Once we arrived, Ruth instructed me to check the list to see which courtroom we were in. I scanned the list a number of times; it was clear that we were not on it. We trooped down to the court registry where we found out that Ruth had failed to file the trial certificate, which was her job as the plaintiff's lawyer. No trial certificate meant no trial. It would be at least another year before the Nottinghams could get a new trial date.

Everyone was of course very upset, as they had waited for this day for quite some time. The only person who did not appear to be upset was Ruth. Did she not file it on purpose? Was that why she did virtually no preparation?

Ruth announced that she was going to take the week off, as she was suddenly free, and then she disappeared, leaving me to console Mrs. Nottingham, after which I went back to the office and told John that no matter what happened, I was taking the next weekend off to be with my children.

I did take the weekend off, planning to spend time with my children; however, aside from attending Morgan and Mitchell's soccer game, I did not see a great deal of my children, as they had made plans with their friends. When I expressed my disappointment that we were not going to have much family time, Sarah pointed out that I had not given them enough notice that I would be home. They had gotten used to my working weekends and had become good at organizing their time without me. It dawned on me that this was a mixed blessing. Obviously, I had brought up rather self-sufficient children, which was a good thing, but I still wanted to be needed for more than money and food. Had I struck the right balance? I supposed only time would tell.

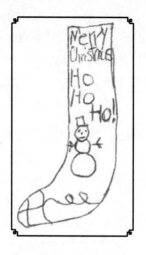

Chapter Four

December
Hall v. Hall

W hen Mr. Hall came to see John McWilliams, he and his wife had been living separate and apart, albeit in the same house, for four years. John had me sit in for the second appointment, because, he said, it was an interesting case and I would learn from it. It did not take long for me to realize that John had lost interest and had me there so that he could introduce me to Mr. Hall and then pass the case off to me.

It was not unusual to hear John berating a client. He certainly did not suffer fools gladly, and, in his view, Mr. Hall and his wife were silly, foolish people who were so caught up in the minute details of life that they did not see the big picture. He advised Mr. Hall that I would be assisting with his case and then basically left it to me to "sort these people out."

When they had separated but decided to stay in the same house, the Halls did up a cohabitation agreement. This agreement stated that from that time on they would be roommates, as there was no longer an intimate nature to the relationship. They did acknowledge that they shared two children and "while the romantic nature of their relationship no longer existed, the children did."

The agreement set out the daily, weekly, and monthly chores for which each party was responsible. The details listed in the agreement included such things as who washed the baby bottle parts, who was responsible for washing the cat box, and who watered the outdoor plants. It went into great detail as to who would pay for what and which parts of the house each could use, depending on certain circumstances and the time of day.

What the agreement did not provide for was the major issues: custody, access, child support, spousal support, and division of assets. Mr. Hall had come to see John because the parties now wanted to sell the house and go their separate ways, mainly because Mrs. Hall had met a man with whom she did have an intimate relationship.

Mrs. Hall had consulted a lawyer who had commenced and served Mr. Hall with an application seeking an order that Mrs.

Hall have interim sole possession of the house, interim sole custody, and interim child support.

An interim application is one that is brought prior to a trial and is, on the face of it, one that seeks an order in the interim or until matters are finally settled either by a trial or a settlement. However, particularly when you are dealing with orders pertaining to children, it is often very difficult to change the provisions of an interim order. Once there has been an order that gives one party interim custody judges are generally reluctant to change the children's residence. Accordingly, interim orders are very important, as they provide for a status quo, which is an uphill battle to change.

As an articling student, I was not allowed to argue a contested application, but, in John's view, I could take care of all the preparation for him to appear in court. Because interim custody was at issue, we needed not only Mr. Hall's sworn statement, called an affidavit, but affidavits from friends and family supporting his position.

One would think that after four years of sharing custody in the same house, it would be reasonable to continue shared or joint custody when the Halls moved to separate residences. That line of thinking assumes that people will be reasonable. Many are not. All sorts of factors come into play. In the Halls' case, Mr. Hall was afraid that his wife's new man would usurp his role as father to their two young children. It appeared, from her material, that Mrs. Hall did want to form a nuclear family with her new partner, with Mr. Hall having a minimal role in the children's lives.

Mr. Hall was in a catch-22 position. He would be happy with joint custody and wanted to file material showing how well the shared custody had worked for four years. Mrs. Hall wanted sole custody and, from her initial material, was clearly prepared to argue that she was the better parent, Mr. Hall was a terrible parent, and joint custody would not work. Mr. Hall had to defend himself against his wife's allegations, but in doing so, it would give a judge a snapshot of a couple who could not get along well enough to make joint custody work.

While I was going over the options with Mr. Hall in John's office, John stormed in shouting that the contractor did not know what he was doing and that Ruth's interior design ideas were ridiculous. Mr. Hall, who was a soft-spoken, precise accountant, looked appalled and somewhat frightened by this outburst. When I pointed out to John that I had a client, he roared into Ruth's office next door and continued his rant, which was perfectly audible to Mr. Hall and me.

The argument between Ruth and John as to how the office should be constructed and decorated was one that Ruth, who was putting up most of the money, usually won. All who worked there, along with some of the clients, knew that Ruth was paying for most of the renovations, as she brought it up in most of their screaming matches.

Neither John nor Ruth had an overall plan for the office. This meant that walls were constructed and then torn down, sometimes after they had been painted. It also meant that wiring was changed, which in some cases meant that computers were unplugged and information lost.

The longer I was there, the more sympathetic I felt toward the contractor and tradesmen. However, the renovations were being done on a cost-plus basis, so no doubt the contractor was laughing all the way to the bank. Every time Ruth and John changed their minds, the cost of the project escalated.

As well as getting the material ready for the Hall application, John had advised me that I was in charge of the Christmas party. This was an event that the firm had each year, to which most family law lawyers plus a number of judges were invited. I was told that it was an open house, which started at about 4:00 p.m. and apparently ended when the last man or woman was left standing. In other words, along with the plates of hors d'oeuvres, the liquor flowed freely.

Once again, Caroline came to my rescue. Although she did not have a lot of time to actually organize the party, she was able to give me an idea of numbers and what had been done in other years. Caroline was particularly busy, since, in addition to all her other work, the edict had come down from our leader that she was to do all of my work on the Hall file.

Because the office was so chaotic, Caroline and I decided that we would go for a drink after work so that she could outline what had to be done to pull off the party. Apparently, while Caroline and I were at the bar planning the party and having many laughs at the expense of our workmates, Ruthless spotted us from the table she was sharing with her husband. The next day, she took me aside and told me that it was not appropriate for me to be drinking with the staff. She did not say why, but the implication was that it was as unseemly as the gardener eating at the same table as the lord of the manor.

As Caroline was my favourite person in the office by far, I had no intention of not going for a drink with her whenever I pleased. We were both single parents, so we did not have time to get together very often, but when we did, we always had a good time. As well as being incredibly bright, Caroline had a wicked sense of humour and a photographic memory, which, one evening after a few drinks, she described as a photogenic memory. A few years after my articling year, Caroline went to law school. She is now practising law in a small community and enjoying a lifestyle that she always wanted.

The Christmas party involved a fair amount of work, made worse by the fact that Ruth, who contributed absolutely nothing, kept second-guessing everything I did, starting with the invitations. Every day for about two weeks Ruth gave me a new sketch of what she wanted on the invitation. As she had no artistic ability, it was usually difficult even to discern what she meant. The party was to be on December 23. By December 12, I simply had to get something to the printers, so I made an executive decision, incorporating one or two of Ruth's ideas, and sent it to the printers.

The printers, who had done the firm's invitations for years, put a rush on the job, and we had the finished product by December 16. Ruth, of course, was not happy with them, but there wasn't much she could do about it except complain. I never told her that the drawing on the front of the card had been done by my daughter, who was very good at that sort of thing. I felt bad that I could not give Sarah the credit, but I knew that if I did, Ruth would be put out that her daughter, who was 19, had not been involved.

Ruth felt it would be nice if every invitation was signed by her and John. Fortunately, John was not interested, "As that stupid woman suggested," in signing 200 invitations, as he was busy practising law, "Unlike that stupid woman!"

Having avoided that hurdle, Caroline and I stayed after work so we could get the invitations in the mail. Caroline typed the envelopes, and I stuffed the envelopes and affixed the stamp. The process took about three hours, if you included the hour we spent rewarding ourselves at the bar next door.

Next, we had to figure out decorations and where to put it all in an office that was basically a construction zone. With much input from Ruth, which we simply ignored, and arguments between Ruth and John as to whether or not there should be a Christmas tree, the party happened.

Just about everyone we invited came to the event; some just dropped in, while the hard-core drinkers stayed to the bitter end, as did Caroline and I. We felt we had to stay to make sure that those who had over-imbibed did not drive their cars. Some turned their car keys over to us with little fuss; those who were determined to drive, in some cases, had to be literally wrestled to the ground.

After the last drunk was on his way, Caroline and I sat down and had our first drink of the evening. Up until then, we knew we had to keep our wits about us, so we could keep the food coming and the drinks flowing and break up several heated arguments, one of which turned into a knockdown, drag-out fight.

Observing some of the particularly sloppy drunks, I was again reminded of the "cream of the crop" remark of the Chief Justice on the first day of law school. I guess he had never attended a McWilliams Cameron Christmas party.

One of the traditions at McWilliams Cameron was to give the employees—Patrick and me, each of the secretaries, Jazmin, and the bookkeeper—a turkey at Christmas. John, of course, ordered the biggest turkeys he could find. This was our Christmas bonus, a tradition I presume he borrowed from the Dickens classic *A Christmas Carol*.

Aside from Caroline and me, the other recipients of a large, heavy, frozen bird lived alone, and all but Patrick rode the bus to work. No problem—the "baby lawyer" would pick up and deliver the turkeys. I ended up spending Christmas Eve delivering turkeys to people who had no use for them. Most, in the spirit of Christmas and because they did not have a freezer that would accommodate such a large bird, donated their Christmas "bonus" to the food bank.

The only people who felt good about the turkeys were John, Ruth, the food bank, and me. It was a silly, ill-conceived tradition that made the partners feel they had helped all the "Bob Cratchets" who worked for them.

I made sure that my turkey was the first to be delivered so that my children could spend the afternoon defrosting it. They did a good job. When I got home on Christmas Eve, my 30-pound Christmas bonus was floating in the bathtub, with my children and some of their friends adding hot water from time to time. Apparently, our turkey entertained a number of the neighbourhood's 11-year-old boys, who pretty well soaked themselves and the bathroom in their attempt to defrost it before I got home.

By morning, the bird was ready to be cooked. Even though I had my parents and my two sisters and their families for Christmas dinner, we had enough turkey left for a number of dinners and sandwiches, which I froze for school lunches and eventually soup. We also had photographs of my Christmas bonus floating in the bathtub, sitting on the toilet, having a shower, hanging from the shower rod, and dressed in a number of outfits, some of which included my daughter's bras and panties. The boys thought the photos were hilarious; my daughter was not amused.

Although at the time I would have preferred cash, my boys certainly had a lot of fun with the turkey, whom, for no apparent reason, they had named George. The story of George, with accompanying photographs, comes up every year and has become part of our Christmas tradition. Perhaps the fun they had and still have with the retelling of the adventures of George the turkey was, in the long run, better than cash.

Diane Tupper

Chapter Five

January
Fernando v. Fernando

Mr. Fernando was 59 years of age and had seven children with two different women. There was nothing odd about that, as many men have had two consecutive relationships. Mr. Fernando, however, who was quite up front about his situation, had two relationships at the same time—one with Eve, with whom he had three children, and one with Jenny, with whom he had four children.

He managed to keep both relationships going by telling both women that he was a salesman who had to travel out of town. Mr. Fernando was quite wealthy, and the only job he really had was managing his investments. He simply alternated households on a two- to three-week basis.

After about 12 years, the women found out about each other when Mr. Fernando had a heart attack and both "wives" were notified and went to the hospital. Mr. Fernando, who had managed for years to keep the two families separated, had for some unknown reason listed both women as his emergency contact.

Mr. Fernando's heart attack was not serious, but the ramifications of his hospital stay were. He had gone through a marriage ceremony with both women but was only legally married to Eve, whom he had married first, six months before his "marriage" to Jenny.

Both women, after they had dealt with their disbelief, were understandably outraged and devastated, particularly Jenny, when she learned that she was not legally married to her "husband" of 12 years.

Mr. Fernando really did not seem to understand what all the fuss was about. He explained that he loved both women and all seven children. He genuinely appeared to believe that once Eve and Jenny got used to the situation, life could go on as usual.

John had called me into his office as soon as he got the gist of Mr. Fernando's story. As in other instances, John's reason for having me there, according to him, was because it would be a good learning experience. In this case, I think he simply wanted someone to hear the story with him so that we could laugh about it over an after-work drink.

John had practiced law for more than 20 years and thought he had seen every possible set of facts, but this was a situation he had never dealt with. In one case, we had both a married and a common-law couple. The law that governed both relationships was quite different, and John immediately sent me off to research the applicable legislation and case law.

While we were meeting with Mr. Fernando and explaining his options, his wives, rather than retaining lawyers, arranged to meet one another. They found that not only did they have a husband in common and children who had half brothers and sisters, they also were very much alike and, in fact, immediately liked each other.

After their initial shock and anger, both Eve and Jenny decided that neither of them wanted to lose Mr. Fernando. He was very generous and good to his children. They both had the luxury of staying home with their children, and they both had become used to having time to themselves when Mr. Fernando was "working out of town." Much to our surprise, Eve and Jenny decided that they simply wanted life to continue as usual.

Although we were happy for all concerned, to be truthful, John and I were exceedingly disappointed that we no longer had this intriguing case. What we did have was a good story to tell over drinks at the bar next door.

That bar was a meeting place for a number of lawyers. John went there almost every night after work and usually tried to persuade me to go with him. He was never in any hurry to go home, but I was. At first, I found it difficult to say no; after all, he was my boss. However, as time went by, being with my children became more important than pleasing John, who really just wanted an audience to listen to his stories.

As it was, I felt that I was losing my resolution to keep a reasonable balance between work and children. By the time I got home and dealt with dinner, homework, and driving the twins to their soccer and baseball practices and games, I had no energy left to simply spend downtime with them. What I, and all single mothers needed, was a wife.

Sarah wanted to get a part-time job to make some money for the clothes that she felt she desperately needed. Although money was tight, I proposed that she work for me. She would be responsible for making dinner, doing the laundry, and keeping the house generally tidy. This served two purposes: it helped me, and it meant that she would be occupied after school. After some bargaining over what she should be paid, Sarah agreed to be my "wife."

We had a family meeting where I made it clear to Morgan and Mitchell that Sarah was not their slave and that they were responsible for their own rooms, taking out the garbage, and cleaning up after themselves. After further discussions, I agreed to raise the boys' allowance, which they would only receive if they kept their end of the bargain.

Although things did not always run smoothly, the new division of labour worked fairly well. It meant that I could spend more time on the weekends with my children, except, of course, on the weekends that I had to work, usually because Ruth or John had left trial preparation to the last minute.

There were some advantages to working on the weekend. I had a desk and a chair; the renovators did not work on the weekend; and I could help myself to the office supplies, which Jazmin very reluctantly handed out during the week. If I asked her for a pencil, she would want to know what had happened to the one she had given me two weeks ago. She apparently counted the dictation tapes, as every so often, she would circulate a memo about unaccounted-for tapes.

Everyone, except Patrick, but including John and Ruth, tiptoed around Jazmin. I never did learn why. She was formidable-looking with her upswept bleached-blond hair, which never moved; her long, bright-red fingernails; and her ample bosom, which also never moved.

Our bookkeeper, Jacquelynn, was another employee who was somewhat of a mystery. Unlike Jazmin, she was friendly and easy to get along with but was borderline incompetent at her job. Because I had been a bookkeeper before I went to law school, Jacquelynn would often come to me with her bookkeeping problems. I soon learned that she had very little understanding of bookkeeping but simply did the books by rote.

The previous bookkeeper had left Jacquelynn with a set of instructions on how to use Simply Accounting. She could follow the instructions as long as nothing new came up and there were no errors. If there was a problem, she was lost, and I would have to sort out the books for her. I realized how little she understood about her job when she asked me one day if I could explain to her the difference between a debit and a credit.

I never did learn how Jacquelynn got the job and kept it. I did learn, while correcting her mistakes, that she made more money than I did and enjoyed six weeks' holiday per year and a generous number of sick days, which she took on a regular basis.

No one ever told me whether or not I was entitled to holidays, and I never asked. Accordingly, I worked the whole year with no time off, save and except for a few hours here and there to deal with a family crisis, usually involving the twins. They injured themselves so often I was on a first-name basis with the emergency staff at our local hospital.

Morgan broke his arm when he fell off the school roof, which he had climbed up to retrieve a ball. Mitchell broke his collarbone twice playing baseball. Both times, he was playing catcher and lunged over home plate to tag the runner. Both times, he tagged the runner out when the runner ran into him.

The twins' most spectacular accident happened when they were playing tag at school. Morgan and Mitchell, who were running opposite ways around the school, ran into each other. Morgan broke his jaw, and Mitchell needed 20-odd stitches to repair his face from the impact of his brother's jaw and teeth.

In addition, both boys had several sprains, several sets of stitches, and a black eye each, which they sustained from some kind of game of chicken.

While the boys' injuries were a result of their daredevil behaviour, Sarah's only injuries were incurred in the pursuit of beauty. In the summer, she blistered her face by lying in the sun under a homemade tinfoil contraption. In January, she bleached her hair to the consistency of straw. The only "cure" for her hair was to cut it very short. I thought the new cut suited her, whereas she thought it was a disaster from which she would never recover.

Financially, I received a bit of a boost in January because the Family Maintenance Enforcement Program finally got to my file. FMEP is the program that enforces child support orders where the payer is not paying. On January 15, I received my first cheque as a result of the garnishee that had been sent to my former husband's employer. As long as he did not change jobs, the garnishee stayed in place for a year. Finally, my children's father was contributing—albeit unwillingly—to their support. Because he had not paid for three years, the garnishee was for ongoing support plus a contribution toward the arrears of child support.

Altogether I was receiving $550 per month, which more than paid for the cost of Sarah's help and the boys' allowance. It meant that there was a little money for extras, such as the odd dinner out, movies for the kids, and wine for mum.

Sadly, it meant that my former husband saw even less of our children; he claimed that because of the garnishee, he was too poor to put gas in his car or to take them anywhere.

Diane Tupper

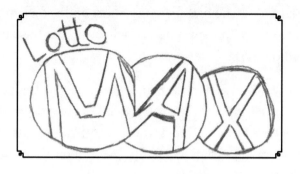

Chapter Six

February
Cameron v. Cameron

*I*n family law, there are three "triggering events": a divorce, a separation agreement, or a declaration by the court that there is no possibility of reconciliation. The assets that exist at the time of the triggering event are family assets that are to be shared between the parties. Any assets acquired by either party after the triggering event are that party's sole property, unless family assets were used to buy the property.

Ruth Cameron was, of course, well aware of the ramifications of a triggering event, but she was adamant that I find a way around it.

She and her husband had been separated for about four months. Three days after she had me go to court and get a declaration that there was no prospect of reconciliation, her husband won $4.5 million in the lottery.

Ruthless was beside herself. Somehow, in her distraught state, she felt it was my fault for getting the order, which she had asked me to get. If only I had waited another week, the lottery winnings would be a family asset. Never mind that she had told me to get the order immediately.

Once she somewhat calmed down, she wanted me to find a way around the untimely triggering event. I tried. I thought that if the funds that were used to buy the ticket came from a joint account, we might have an argument. They did not. Ruth had always insisted on separate bank accounts.

I spent the better part of a week researching every case where lottery winnings, or any other windfall, such as an inheritance, were involved. Although Ruthless was sure there must be some way around it, the law was very clear. The only argument that I felt might have a chance was that because her husband had won a considerable amount of money, there was a chance that a court might reapportion the family assets in Ruth's favour rather than dividing them evenly.

I could not find a case to back up my argument, but I thought it was worth a try if the matter went to court. I also suggested that perhaps Ruth's husband might agree to an uneven split in light of his lottery winnings. In Canada, lottery winnings are not taxable, so he would receive all of the $4.5 million.

The Camerons had considerable assets. Dr. Cameron was a successful medical doctor, a surgeon who specialized in neurosurgery. Ruth Cameron had practised law for all of her working life. Between them, they had acquired a big house in an exclusive neighbourhood, condos in Whistler and Hawaii, as well as various investments and Registered Retirement Savings Plans as well as Ruth's partnership interest in McWilliams Cameron.

This was not a case where one party had met someone else. Dr. Cameron simply wanted out. I suspect that he had only stayed as long as he had because of their children, both of whom were now grown and had places of their own. Ruthless was a very difficult woman, and I think Dr. Cameron had had enough of her craziness.

John McWilliams was Ruth's lawyer, but I was the one who had to listen to her, as John simply did not have the patience. Her main concern was not that she was losing her husband of 30 years. Her focus was on the money—having to divide their assets and her anger about the lottery money.

Ruth tried to alienate her children from their father. She telephoned them at home and at work and turned up at their offices and homes unannounced. I knew what she was doing, because she told me over long lunches, which I was forced to endure. I had little choice, as she was my boss and she apparently had no friends—at least none that were willing to sit for hours listening to her hold forth on how unfair her situation was and how poor she was going to be.

Poor, of course, is a relative term. Ruth's idea of poor was most peoples' idea of comfortably off. It was hard for me, who supported myself and three children, having listened to the amount Ruth spent simply on entertainment, to feel much empathy toward her.

Ruth using up my time in this fashion was not only tiring and boring, it also meant that I was not billing other files. Like lawyers at most law firms, I was given a number of hours that I should be billing each month. As I could not bill Ruth for all the time she spent ranting to me about her problems, I was working weekends trying to bill my monthly quota. This meant that I was spending less time with my children, who had too many unsupervised hours.

The only way I could see to restore the balance between work and children was to settle the Cameron case. I suspected that Dr. Cameron, whom I had met on a number of occasions, was likely keen to settle matters between him and Ruth quickly. Ruthless was also calling him nonstop at work and home, screaming how unfair and greedy he was being.

As an articling student, I could not conduct a settlement conference, so I suggested (basically begged) John to conduct one. It took some persuading as John had done his best to avoid Ruth as much as he could. He finally agreed, but only if I would contact everyone and pick a day that worked with his calendar.

It took some time. First of all, I had to persuade Ruth that she could sit in the same room as her husband. Then I had to contact Dr. Cameron's lawyer and get his and his client's agreements and available dates. Both John and Dr. Cameron's lawyer had busy schedules, as did Dr. Cameron, but I was persistent and personally motivated. I needed to spend more time with my children and less with Ruth.

I finally got everyone's agreement to meet at our office on February 14, forgetting at the time that this was Valentine's Day. Surprisingly, I was the only one who seemed to appreciate the irony of meeting on this particular date. I did tell our bookkeeper, who liked to decorate the office for every occasion, to tone down the hearts and flowers and not to put any decorations in the boardroom where we were to meet.

John had me sit in at the settlement conference, partly, I am sure, because he had paid no attention to either the issues or the assets in question. The only issue was division of property. Spousal support was a nonissue as both parties' earnings were about the same, and with the children being self-sufficient, there was no issue as to custody or child support.

In preparation for the meeting, Dr. Cameron's lawyer and I had obtained appraisals of the three properties and Ruth's interest in McWilliams Cameron and ascertained the value of the Camerons' various investments and RRSPs. Altogether, their assets were worth about $3.5 million. In addition, of course, Dr. Cameron had his lotto winnings of $4.5 million.

Much to everyone's surprise, Dr. Cameron agreed to give Ruth all of their combined assets because he had his lottery winnings. This was a very generous offer under the circumstances and certainly much better than Ruth would end up with after a trial. But Ruth being Ruthless was not happy because her husband would have more money than she would.

John recommended that she accept Dr. Cameron's offer right then and there. Having practised law for a long time, John knew that the party who wanted out of the marriage was often feeling guilty and tended to be more generous at first. But guilt fades, and after a while, the person who instigated the breakup becomes less generous. John also wanted her to settle because if they went to court, Ruth's interest in the law firm would be at issue and the value of it would be public knowledge.

After a couple of days of reflection and persuasion by John, Ruth reluctantly agreed to the terms of the settlement. The only assets left to be divided were household contents, which one would think, considering the rather large sums of money each would receive, should not be a problem. Not so. The Camerons squabbled and bickered over a number of items, some of which had very little monetary value.

As I mentioned earlier, it is not unusual in family law for the parties to settle the big items but haggle over small, relatively inexpensive items. It is, I believe, a matter of not wanting to completely let go or break their connection. I have seen people pay their lawyers $350 per hour to squabble over who will copy family photos and who gets pots and pans, cleaning supplies, and—my personal favourite—a home blood pressure machine.

I have also witnessed clients who want their lawyers to go to court over petty, mean, and downright silly claims, such as access to the family cat. I had one client who wanted me to go to court and argue for half of the china that had been in his wife's family for three generations. Another man wanted me to go to court with an application that he would get the family's only TV set, the one his children watched at their mom's house.

The worst are clients who want to punish the other party by using the children. One father, who had his son every second weekend, refused to take him to his soccer games since his mother had registered him. This not only punished mum but also his son and his son's team.

Then there are the parents who run down the other party to their child or children. I have tried to explain to clients that by doing this to the other parent, they are, by extension, lowering the child's self-image. Telling a child that his mum or dad is useless, stupid, lazy, etc., is mean and childish and, often, in the long run, backfires. I know from personal experience how hard it is at times to keep your mouth shut, but unless the other party is a dangerous criminal, talking down about a child's parent has absolutely no upside.

My children, especially the boys, made all sorts of excuses for their father—he could not afford gas; he had to work a lot; his car was always breaking down and he could not afford a new one, as he had to pay me money. I understood that they made these excuses because they did not want to face the fact that their father simply did not want to see them enough to make an effort. Still, it was very hard to keep my mouth shut even when Sarah, who saw through his excuses, stated that she did not care if she ever saw him. Of course she cared, but she had been disappointed so many times that she had quit hoping. It broke my heart. It also added to my guilt, for, after all, I had picked this man to marry and be the father of my children.

The lack of an involved father made it even more important that I maintain a balance of sorts between work and my children. Fortunately, I had played a lot of sports in my youth and, despite my advanced age, could still shoot hoops, catch a baseball, and kick a soccer ball with my boys. I treasured those moments, as I knew that soon they would not be caught dead playing soccer with their mom.

Chapter Seven

March
Bar Exams

During your articling year, you are required to take a month of classes to prepare for the bar exams. After you have taken the classes, you sit for two days of exams, which cover different areas of law. The law firm that you are working for is supposed to give you the month off to attend the classes, study, and take the exams.

The classes and exams are given by lawyers through Continuing Legal Education, whose building happened to be across the street from McWilliams Cameron. Because of the proximity, John saw no reason why I could not work in between and before and after classes. As I was hoping that John would hire me after my articling year, in spite of all the chaos, I did not argue with him or stand up for myself. What I did do was work and study incredibly long hours that month in order to pass the bar exams and, at the same time, bill as many hours as possible.

In the month of March, I basically only went home to shower, sleep for about five hours, change my clothes, and make sure that my children were still alive and well. The children were great. After I explained my schedule to them, they rose to the occasion with only the odd complaint. Sarah bought the groceries, cooked dinner, did the laundry, and kept the house reasonably tidy. Morgan and Mitchell did their regular chores but also made their school lunches and did the vacuuming—in a hit-and-miss manner—but it was better than nothing.

My children helped me make it through the month without having a breakdown. I was, and continue to be, very grateful for and proud of their contributions. Of course, it probably helped that I promised the boys the latest PlayStation and Sarah a cell phone if they upped their game.

What to wear, although not my biggest difficulty, was a bit of a conundrum. The other students wore informal clothes, mostly jeans and running shoes. Because I was working for part of every day, I needed to wear business clothes to the office. As I already stood out, being 20-odd years older than most of the students, in a pathetic and time-consuming attempt to fit in, for the first few days, I changed my clothes each time I went from classes to the office. As some days I went back and forth several times, I quickly realized this simply took too much time. For the rest of the month, I stayed in my office clothes all day and gave up trying to fit in.

In any event, I had very little time to worry about how I looked. John and Ruth continued to give me mounds of work and pawn off clients that they did not want to handle. A number of the clients I inherited turned out to have interesting and memorable cases.

One of the clients John sent my way was Mrs. Henderson. Her former husband, a veterinarian, had managed to avoid paying child support for three years. There was an outstanding order for $1,500 per month, but Dr. Henderson made it hard to collect from him. At one point, we had obtained a garnishing order naming him as the garnishee. He immediately incorporated, which meant we would have to start the process all over again and get an order garnishing his company.

Unlike the majority of clients, Mrs. Henderson never whined or complained, but she was in serious debt and was in danger of losing her house. She needed the child support, but she could not afford legal fees.

An unconventional solution came to me in the middle of the night. I telephoned Mrs. Henderson the next day and explained my idea to her. I told her she must not tell anyone that it came from me, as I was not sure how the Law Society would view my approach.

Dr. Henderson's clinic was situated on a main, extremely busy road. Two days after I shared my idea with her, Mrs. Henderson was seen picketing her former husband's office, pushing a stroller, and carrying a sign that read, "DR. HENDERSON

DOES NOT PAY HIS CHILD SUPPORT." Two days later, Mrs. Henderson received a letter by courier, enclosing a cheque for all of the back child support and 12 postdated cheques for the upcoming year.

Solving Mrs. Henderson's dilemma gave me an inordinate amount of satisfaction. I had helped a likeable, uncomplaining client at no cost to her by simply thinking outside the box. Rather than a legal solution, her problem was solved by a simple common-sense approach. The fact that a photograph of Mrs. Henderson picketing made the local paper probably guaranteed that Dr. Henderson would continue to keep his child support payments up-to-date.

I had another case that month that had a very unhappy ending and showed how far some people will go to hurt their former spouse. A term of the Cunninghams' separation agreement was that Mr. Cunningham would maintain $200,000 worth of life insurance, with Mrs. Cunningham as the beneficiary for as long as he was to pay spousal support—in his case, six years.

The life insurance policy had the standard clause that the policy was null and void if Mr. Cunningham committed suicide within the first year of the policy. Incredibly, Mr. Cunningham actually killed himself one day before the year was up, leaving his former wife with no spousal support or insurance.

I had heard other clients say that they would rather die than give their estranged spouse money. I always classified these threats in the same category as those of clients who said they would rather spend every last cent on legal fees than share their assets with the person they had sworn to cherish until death parted them. Mr. Cunningham really meant it. Unimaginably, death to him was a better option than sharing with his wife of 26 years.

In March, I also met with a potential client who had an immense self-induced dilemma. About 10 years before he came to see me, he and his wife had obtained a divorce in order to reduce their income tax. At that time, child support was deductible by the payer and taxable in the hands of the person who received it. Accordingly, if the payer, usually the husband, made more money than the payee, the "divorced family" as a whole paid less income tax than the intact family.

The Lee family continued to live together after they got their divorce in the same house as husband and wife. The Lees now wanted a real divorce as well as a division of assets and an agreement with respect to custody, access, and child support. The problem was that they were already divorced and had been committing income-tax fraud for 10 years.

We did not take Mr. Lee's case, as we did not want any part of the Lees' fraudulent behaviour. Not only had they committed income tax fraud, but they had committed perjury by telling the court, as part of their divorce application, that there had been no prospect of reconciliation and then continued to live together. I don't know what happened to the Lees, who were an outstanding example of what happens to those who weave the proverbial "tangled web."

I believe that most family law clients do not purposely lie to their lawyers, but they do tend to exaggerate the other party's shortcomings and their own lack of culpability. Some clients have nothing good to say about the person they chose to marry not realizing how this attitude reflects upon them.

In Canada, we have no-fault divorce; it is a concept that many clients find hard to grasp. Who left whom or who did what to whom does not affect the division of assets or the amount of support. The only time that a person's behaviour is relevant is with respect to issues regarding custody and access to children and then only if the behaviour is such that it would be harmful to the children. Many clients are outraged that their spouse can leave them for someone else and still be entitled to half of their assets.

Because of this, some clients try to cheat their spouse by hiding assets, usually in undisclosed bank accounts. I did act for one woman, who accumulated and hid cash, quite a lot of cash presumably for a rainy day. It was only by accident that her husband discovered his wife's stash. The money was hidden in empty soup, vegetable, and fruit cans, which she washed after using the contents; it was money she had skimmed from her housekeeping allowance and removed from her husband's wallet.

This woman kept the cans of cash in plain sight in her kitchen cupboard. She told me later that she felt quite safe leaving the money on the kitchen shelves, as her husband did not cook and never went into the cupboards. This changed when they started living separately in the same house and the wife quit cooking for her husband. Sick of fast food, one day, the husband decided he could probably handle heating up some canned soup. Imagine his surprise, and his wife's dismay, when he found what was really in the soup, fruit, and vegetable cans—altogether $157,000. Clearly, the more common under-the-mattress hiding spot would have been a better choice.

As well as clients who hid assets, I encountered a few who got back at the other party by destroying their belongings. One client, whose husband had left her for a much younger woman, took out her anger by cutting the crotch out of all of her husband's pants. Another threw all her husband's clothes into the backyard and then poured bleach over his entire wardrobe.

During my articling year, we had a husband who was quite sure his wife was having an affair with her personal trainer. She was. He followed her one night to a motel where she was meeting her new love. While she was in the motel, someone slashed the tires of her car and the lover's car and threw about a dozen eggs at each car.

Nothing can bring insanity to the lives of otherwise reasonable people like a nasty divorce. The saying, "Hell hath no fury like a woman scorned," in fairness, should also refer to men, as I have seen both men and woman exhibit unimaginably petty, crazy, immature behaviour. Apparently, there is nothing new about this behaviour; according to my research, the phrase was coined by William Congreve in 1697.

As well as telling us we were the cream of the crop in his address on the first day of law school, the Chief Justice had said, "Look left. Look right. One of you will not be here at the end of law school." I had managed to make it through law school, but one cannot practice law unless one passes the bar exams, and with my crazy schedule, I was seriously concerned about passing.

The only time I had to study was late at night and on the odd weekend. There simply was not enough time to digest all of the material. With only five days to go before I had to write the exams, I was in full panic mode and made a decision of which I am not particularly proud. I phoned the office saying I was too sick to come in, and then I telephoned Sarah's school and told them she was too sick to come to school.

I needed Sarah to help me study. For two long days, Sarah sat with my notes while I recited what I could remember in each subject. If I missed a point, Sarah would mark it with red ink and we would go over it again, and again. We took the odd bathroom and eating break, but other than that, we studied for two 12-hour days.

Sarah never complained. I think she quite enjoyed marking me wrong and pointing out the information I had missed. Morgan and Mitchell did complain, as they thought it was unfair that Sarah got to skip school, even though I explained to them that Sarah was working way longer hours than she ever did when she attended school. There is absolutely no doubt that I passed the bar exams because of the time my daughter spent listening to and correcting me until I had absorbed the material. Sarah certainly earned her cell phone and my undying gratitude.

Chapter Eight

April
Foster v. Fischer

Once I had made it through March and passed the bar exams, I was relieved and exhausted. I also felt incredibly guilty, as, aside from the two-day studying marathon with Sarah, I had spent virtually no time with my children. I had not attended any of Morgan and Mitchell's soccer games, nor had I monitored their homework. I had also missed one of Sarah's dance recitals, although I had found time to send her a single red rose with a card urging her to "break a leg," which I am thankful she did not.

I scheduled an appointment with Morgan and Mitchell's teacher, Mr. Whiteside, who was young and called me "ma'am." The boys had failed to complete a rather complicated project, which obviously needed parent participation. Other than this project, most of their homework had been done and turned in, albeit often late and sometimes incomplete.

Mr. Whiteside spoke to me as if I were the same age as the student who usually sat in the desk I was crammed into. When I tried to explain my crazy March schedule, he responded as if I had just used the excuse, "The dog ate my homework." He told me, in the same tone I am sure he used with his students, that each child had a journal in which he set out the day's homework and that parents were supposed to check it over.

Of course I knew about the journals, which my sons had been bringing home every day for five years, but in March, I had been lucky if I'd seen my sons, never mind their journals. The interview ended with me promising to do better and assuring Mr. Whiteside that Morgan and Mitchell and I would complete the missed project.

At least I thought that the meeting had ended. It had not. Mr. Whiteside wanted some legal advice. After two years of marriage, his wife had left him for the gym teacher. He had a whole barrage of questions, which he had apparently written out in preparation for my visit to the school.

This was not the first time I had been asked for free legal advice. My hairdresser was going through a messy divorce, and while she had me captive in the chair, she bombarded me with questions and described details of her life that I would rather not know. Relatives and friends sought advice, sometimes for a friend of a friend.

It surprised me that so many people would have the nerve to seek free advice. I am sure that my hairdresser does not give free haircuts to anyone who asks. Nor would my dentist fill my teeth for nothing. But he did not hesitate to ask my advice while my mouth was frozen and gaping open.

There are also the people who ask your advice and then tell you that you are wrong. One friend of a friend had the nerve to ask my opinion and, when I was stupid enough to give it, told me I was wrong because she had seen a similar case on *Judge Judy*. I very quickly learned not to give any advice. For one thing, I was only hearing one side of the story and I did not have all the facts, but mainly I did not want to talk about work during the few hours I was not at the office.

Working at McWilliams Cameron involved tiptoeing around Jazmin, gauging John's mood swings, working around the never-ending renovations, finding a place where I could work, and avoiding Ruth, who could waste hours of my time, usually obsessing about her divorce. As well, of course, there was a steady stream of clients with a wide variety of difficulties and desperate levels of craziness.

One of the most confusing was the *Foster v. Fischer* matter. Initially, it seemed quite straightforward. Mr. Foster made an appointment with John and told him that he wanted a divorce. He said that because his wife also wanted a divorce, he felt that they could settle the issues of division of property, custody, access, and child support by agreement. This sounded way too boring to John, so he passed the file on to me.

As I interviewed Derek Foster, I suspected that he was not telling me the whole story. When I asked him what had precipitated the breakup, he mumbled something to the effect that he and his wife had just grown apart. After much prodding on my part, the full story, over the space of several interviews, finally emerged. For those who read the celebrity gossip magazines, this case was similar to the Shania Twain story, a case where the parties had simply changed partners or had swapped wives.

This case, however, was much more complicated than Shania Twain's for a number of reasons. Twain's husband had left her for her best friend, and quite some time later, she hooked up with her best friend's husband. The Fosters and the Fischers, however, simultaneously decided to switch partners. It was also different in that no one had much money, and both couples had three children.

According to Mr. Foster, all concerned, who were next-door neighbours, decided at a barbeque one night, no doubt after many drinks, that they would be happier with the other party's spouses. Incredibly, the next day, the husbands changed houses and set up housekeeping with the other party's wife. My first thought was how disturbing and confusing this must have been for the children, all of whom were under the age of 10. How does a small child process the fact that Daddy is now living next door with three other children and that Mommy is now sleeping with his or her friend's father? Mr. Foster's view was that the children would adjust without much trouble. He simply did not see the problem.

To make matters more confusing, at least for the four lawyers involved, the children all had somewhat similar names: Katie, Catlin, Kyle, Kent, Cathy, and Kyley. On more than one court application, at least one of the lawyers paired the wrong children with the wrong parents.

As the case progressed, one of the problems that emerged was that all four adults felt entitled to come and go from both houses. Although this was a more complicated situation than most, I have dealt with many instances where the husband leaves his wife but then thinks he can come and go as he pleases. He feels that because he still owns the house, he has a right to enter the house whenever he pleases. He does not have that right. Once one party leaves, even if his or her name is on the title, that person has no more right to enter the house uninvited than he or she would have to enter my house.

Besides the legality of the situation, it can be very emotionally disturbing for the already-distraught wife to have her husband, who has left her, dropping in whenever he pleases We had a hard time with the adults in the Foster/Fischer case, all of whom seemed to feel that they could come and go as they pleased. Mrs. Foster was particularly upset about her husband, who had moved next door, entering her residence uninvited.

After some time had passed, it was clear that Mrs. Foster was not happy with the "wife swapping." She had agreed at the barbecue after many drinks, but in the sober light of day, she was terribly hurt, particularly when she learned that her husband and Mrs. Fischer had been carrying on behind her back for some time. Mr. Fischer was similarly surprised and hurt.

After about eight months, which involved a number of court applications and many drafts of separation agreements, both of the new couples broke up. Apparently, the grass was not greener on the other side of the fence.

After spending a considerable amount of money on legal fees, both couples were forced to sell their houses, neither of which had much equity in them to begin with. Both parties went from owning modest homes, which they could afford, to living in rental accommodations, which were not in the catchment area for the school that the older children were attending.

This was one of the saddest cases I handled. In the end, there were six traumatized children going to new schools and living with single-parent moms, with their dads visiting every second weekend. The wives, who had been stay-at-home moms, now had to work at poorly paid entry-level jobs, with their children in full- and part-time day care, the cost of which took up about one-third of their earnings. This all happened because the four young parents, who were bored and clearly drank too much, thought their problems could be solved if they switched partners. Instead, the switch ended up ruining them financially and confusing and no doubt causing long-lasting insecurity for all or some of the children.

The Foster/Fischer case made me feel better about my own situation. At least my children had lived in the same house since they were born and had been enrolled in the same neighbourhood schools. Their father played a very small role in their lives, but they had uncles, aunts, grandparents, and cousins. And they had me. Despite the present imbalance in the time I spent with them compared to my crazy work hours, I was confident that they knew I would always come home and that I loved them unconditionally.

There was no man in my life during this year, nor had there been in the three years I was in law school. Even if there had been a lineup of potential suitors (which there was not), I had decided when I made the daunting decision to return to school that I could not balance a man as well as school and children.

Diane Tupper

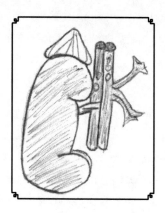

Chapter Nine

May
Capaletti v. Capaletti

*I*t is hard to imagine why Patrick Cunningham chose to practice family law. As I mentioned earlier, he came from a very privileged background, was extremely literal, had no sense of humour, saw the world as black and white, and had no practical common sense. Family law is messy, as there are usually three "truths" or realities: the wife's view, the husband's view, and the truth, which is usually found somewhere in the middle.

A large part of practising family law is finding a practical solution that works for both parties—compromise is usually reached after counselling and/or talking sense to your client. Patrick's response to any dispute was to start his sentence with, "The cases say ..." Certainly, there is a place for case law, particularly if you end up in court, but in the majority of cases, what we do as lawyers is problem solve.

Clients are often not reasonable, particularly when they first separate, especially if they are the one who has been left or replaced. You have to give them a chance to rant, sound off, and sometimes cry. Most clients want to tell you their version of what led up to the separation. When you first meet with a client, in most cases, all you really need to do is listen. They want to tell you their story.

The "no fault" concept is hard for many clients to accept. For instance, the wife, who has worked steadily while being the children's primary caregiver, is never happy to share with the husband, who has worked sporadically, taken little interest in the children, and left her for another woman.

Mrs. Capaletti had every reason to be outraged by the no-fault rules. In November, she gave her alcoholic husband of 28 years one of her kidneys. He subsequently quit drinking, joined a gym, lost 30 pounds, and left her the following April for his 30-year-old personal trainer. In other words, she gave him the gift that would prolong his life, and he chose to spend those extra years with somebody else.

To make matters worse, Mr. Capaletti recovered from the surgery with no complications. Mrs. Capaletti did not. According to her doctor's report, she suffered numerous side effects from the surgery, including infection of the incision, abdominal cramping and pain, high blood pressure, dizziness, and lethargy.

What Mrs. Capaletti wanted was her kidney back or at least removed from her husband's body. At first, that was all I could get her to talk about. She told me about how she fantasized about different ways she could go about this, which included drugging her husband and cutting the kidney out. She seemed to have this so well planned that I began to worry that she might actually try to retrieve her kidney. While I was talking to her, Frank, the plumber, who was working on the pipes just outside the office I was using, stuck his head around the corner and advised us that he had the perfect tool to get her kidney back. I shut the door and hoped that Mrs. Capaletti would not pursue his offer when she left my office.

I tried to talk to her about other issues, but she was fixated on the kidney removal. It was not until I asked her where the kidneys were in the body that she snapped out of her obsession. Neither of us knew exactly where the kidneys were located or what they looked like. This simple fact was the turning point for Mrs. Capaletti. She was able to see the humour in her situation after we had spent some time joking about the hunt for her kidney.

Mrs. Capaletti's situation was a perfect example of why you have to let some clients vent before you can talk about the real issues. Case law is of no use in some cases—listening, asking the right questions, and, many times, finding some humour in an otherwise sad situation is often the way to get your client ready to discuss the real issues.

If you can find something humorous about giving your estranged spouse a kidney, you can probably find something funny or absurd in most cases. Patrick simply lacked the ability to do this and, in fact, was appalled when I told him why Mrs. Capaletti and I were laughing.

There are some cases where the court will reapportion assets in one party's favour. The most common circumstance is when the marriage is short and one party came into the marriage with significantly more assets than the other. The court will sometimes reapportion assets if the husband is unable or unwilling to pay spousal and/or child support.

Mrs. Capaletti did not fall into either of these categories. But she did have the advantage of having an estranged spouse who should feel guilty. From experience, I knew that guilt does not last long, so I advised her that we should make an offer to settle right away. Our offer left Mrs. Capaletti with about two-thirds of the assets and ongoing spousal support. Mr. Capaletti accepted our offer by return. Clearly, the "Kidney-Napper," as my client and I referred to him, did feel guilty.

The Capaletti case illustrates one of the adages that John taught me. Namely, although there are instances where case law is needed, the legal system has far more to do with playing a good hand of poker.

Mrs. Capaletti was one of the rare clients with whom I stayed in touch after her case was settled. Once she recovered from the shock to her body and her emotions, her health slowly improved. She found a part-time job, which used her hobby of photography, and two years later, she remarried. I was invited and attended her wedding, which appeared to be a happy occasion for all concerned, including her two adult children.

At the wedding, her son told me that his dad's relationship with his personal trainer had ended after about a year and that his dad was drinking again. Karma really is a bitch!

There was another client I had in May with whom I have kept in touch, partly because she went to law school after her divorce was final, but mostly because I simply liked her. She was another, albeit younger than Mrs. Capaletti, stay-at-home mom whose husband left her for his much younger secretary. Bobbi Middleton was completely blindsided. She believed she had a solid marriage right up to the day her husband came home from work one night and announced, in front of their 10- and 12-year olds, that he was leaving her to go and live with his secretary.

That night, he packed up some of his clothes and left. The next morning, after a sleepless night, Mrs. Middleton's hair started to fall out. Within about three weeks, she had lost all of her hair, including her eyebrows and eyelashes. Her hair never grew back. She consulted a number of doctors who could not explain the hair loss except to tell her that they had heard of other cases where a shock of some sort had caused permanent hair loss.

She eventually had eyebrows tattooed on and wore wigs and false eyelashes. Bobbi Middleton dealt with the loss of her husband and her hair with a sense of humour that I found admirable. That is not to say that she didn't have some very sad and angry days, but most of the time, she used humour to heal.

She laughed at the cliché of being left for a secretary and the banality of her estranged husband's attempts to look young and "with it." He traded in his "dad car" for a two-seater convertible—not the most usable car in Vancouver, where it rains all year round. When he came to the house to pick up the rest of his things, he was wearing a gold chain—a piece of jewellery that newly separated men seem to favour—and skinny jeans, which did not fit very well over his middle-aged paunch.

Mrs. Middleton told me that she received a lot of sympathetic looks and comments when she wore a scarf rather than a wig. It took her a week or so to realize that people assumed she was a cancer patient who had lost her hair. Her reaction to this mistake was to appreciate that her situation, while difficult, was not life threatening and that time was her friend—not something to be feared. She really understood that time would heal her wound.

What was difficult for Mrs. Middleton to deal with was her husband's lack of interest in his children. He went from being an involved father to an absent one. When he did occasionally see his children, his secretary was always with him, and, according to the two boys, he and the secretary did a lot of hugging and kissing. Anyone who has brought up boys knows that 10- and 12-year-olds find this behaviour both embarrassing and gross.

As there was no room for the boys in the two-seat convertible, Mr. Middleton drove the secretary's pink Volkswagen bug to transport them. The visits were short and unpredictable. Usually, he would take them to McDonald's or, once in a while, to a movie. He quit going to their baseball games and to school events, and he refused to set a schedule for regular visits. Instead, he would usually telephone about half an hour before he planned to pick them up, assuming they would be available.

This is not an unusual problem. A number of access parents that I dealt with refused to work out and/or adhere to a schedule. They want to see their children when it is convenient for them, leaving the custodial parent and the children never knowing in advance when he or she would exercise access. It is, I believe, a control issue, as is the spouse who refuses to give the custodial parent postdated cheques but rather pays monthly, often late, and often only after the custodial parent has asked for the funds. If you do not tell the custodial parent in advance when you are going to see the children, that parent cannot make plans of his or her own. If you deliver support cheques late, the custodial parent is constantly worried about whether and when the cheque will arrive and when he or she can pay the bills.

There is no clear-cut solution to the access and child support games. Some custodial parents, usually mothers, try to dictate terms to the children's dad. One mother I knew told her former husband that he could see the children every second weekend and Wednesday nights. He refused to follow this schedule and wanted to see his children when he chose to, with very little notice. She was then faced with a conundrum; should she stay firm about her schedule, taking the chance that the children would see little of their dad, or should she adjust her and the children's plans every time he called?

Of course, as the children get older, they make their own choices. The dad who has not been a constant in their life usually becomes a low priority in their plans. I had one father complain to me that his former wife had not been helpful in forming his relationship with his children. He was not happy when I pointed out to him that no one can create a relationship for you; with children, you simply have to put in the time and energy.

In contrast, there are the fathers who have little involvement in their children's lives until they are divorced. Then they want to have their children at least 40 percent of the time. This is often a financial decision. The legislation that governs child support states that if the access parent has the children at least 40 percent of the time, he pays less child support.

This term has caused people to keep detailed charts of the time the children are with them. A body of case law has developed over whether you count the hours the children are in school, at dance or swimming lessons, travelling between houses, or sleeping. From the colour-coded, intricate charts I have seen, I suspect that these parents are spending more time documenting who has the children than actually being with them.

I, on the other hand, had none of these access problems, as my former husband hardly ever asked to see our children. I knew this must be hurtful, even though they acted like they didn't care. The boys were still young enough and hopeful enough that they believed their dad would actually come to one of their games as he promised. He never did, but they were still hopeful he would come the next time. Meanwhile, they made excuses for him, as they did not want to believe that he simply did not care.

Sarah now refused to go anywhere with her dad. She was 16 and had little in common with him and no shared experiences.

Spending an hour at McDonald's while her dad asked the questions that distant relatives asked children, such as, "How is school?" and "How tall are you now?" was not her idea of a good time. While the twins like McDonald's, Sarah is into eating healthy food, which does not include a burger and fries.

It broke my heart and added to my guilt for choosing this man to be their father. After all, I tried to involve men in their lives, such as their uncles, but it would never be the same. I knew that their father would not all of a sudden step up to the plate. All I could do was try to be the best parent I could be and try to improve my balancing act.

Diane Tupper

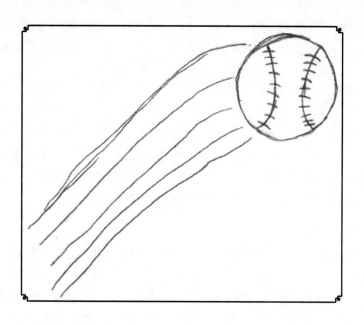

Chapter Ten

June
Adams v. Adams

*I*n June, I learned that, in addition to my extensive caseload, I was expected to be in charge of our softball team. The lawyers in our area had a league, which played in June and July each year. Our law firm had never had a team in the league, but, for some reason, John decided that we should field a team this year.

This decision presented a number of stumbling blocks. We only had a total of 10 employees—four lawyers, Jazmin, Jacquelynn, and four secretaries. Jazmin declined immediately, as did three of the secretaries, who were single moms whose day-care centres closed at 6:00 p.m. So right off the bat we were down to six players; John did not see this as a problem. Even though the rules stated that the players must be employees of the law firm, he saw nothing wrong with giving this rule a broad interpretation and included the incompetent renovators, in particular Jason, one of the plumbers.

Apparently, John knew that Jason had played semipro ball, albeit hardball rather than softball. John, who had played no sports except golf, saw no real difference between the two. To my surprise, Jason wanted to play and was sure he could make the transition. John then had me canvass the rest of the renovators to see if any of them wanted to play. One did; Frank, the plumber, who had also provided Mrs. Capaletti with unsolicited advice on how he would retrieve her kidney.

Even with the two plumbers, we still needed at least one more player. Patrick said that his roommate, Roman, a hairdresser, would play, and Ruth volunteered her son, Peter. Ours was a motley crew and would be playing against large law firms with plenty of lawyers and staff from which to choose.

Our first and only practice was a fiasco, similar in many ways to our disastrous lawyers' meetings. John, Ruth, and Jason argued endlessly over the rules; their arguments were fuelled by the beer that John provided. As the organizer/coach, I suggested that we should defer to Jason, who had actually played ball and who, it quickly became apparent, was considerably more skilled than the rest of us. Both Caroline and I had played softball all through school and could at least throw and catch the ball and, occasionally, hit it. The rest of our team usually got on base only when they were walked or hit by the ball.

Everyone was at least enthusiastic and listened to Jason—with the exception of Ruth and John, who were clearly unable to take part in anything without arguing; they even argued about who would buy the equipment. Some of us had our own gloves, but we needed a few more, as well as batting helmets and equipment for the catcher. After much—and I mean much—discussion, it was decided that those without gloves would buy their own and submit their bills for reimbursement and Jason and I would buy the rest of the equipment. Jason really didn't need me, except for the fact that I had a firm credit card.

The next topic of discussion was uniforms, which we all agreed would simply consist of a T-shirt and player-supplied pants. Of course nothing was simple at McWilliams Cameron. Should the shirt be long or short-sleeved? Should it have a round or a V neckline? Should the firm's name be printed on the shirt? Should the player's name be printed on the shirt? Should we have a team name? Should we have numbers on our shirts? What colour should the shirt be? What colour should the lettering be?

After much discussion and some name-calling, mainly by Ruth and John, it was decided that the shirts would be short-sleeved and dark blue with white lettering. The best name we could come up with was the "Bad News Barristers," which would be printed on the front of the shirts. Our names would be printed on the back with our numbers. As they meant nothing, everyone was allowed to pick his or her own number. For some unknown reason, both Ruth and John wanted the number seven. They reluctantly settled the number issue by the flip of a coin.

Caroline, who had a friend in the T-shirt business, was sent off with me and the credit card to purchase the shirts. We ended up guessing at everyone's size as we could not bear the thought of yet another meeting about the shirts.

As far as who was to play what position, surprisingly, everyone agreed that Jason would make those decisions. Throughout the season, John, Ruth, Patrick, and his roommate all argued with Jason about his assignment of positions and batting order, but Jason refused to be intimidated.

I was in charge of the schedule, which involved yet another set of meetings with representatives from the seven other law firms involved. Apparently, lawyers like to argue and negotiate both in and out of court. Incredibly, it took four meetings to work out a schedule and decide which days we would play. It was finally agreed that games would be on Tuesdays and Thursdays at 6:00 p.m. at a field that had four baseball diamonds. We would play five innings, and each team would play every other team twice, which would equal 14 games. After that, we would have some sort of play-offs.

All of this organization took a substantial amount of time—time that I was not billing clients. Again, I was back to working long hours and weekends in order to bill enough hours. I did, however, see my children most Tuesday and Thursday nights during June and July as they attended most of our baseball games. Although the other lawyers in our firm thought my children's attendance showed their support of their mother, they really came for the amusement value.

All the other teams came from much larger firms, had played in the league for a number of years, and had uniforms that included baseball pants, proper jerseys, matching socks, baseball cleats, and caps. We clearly looked unprofessional as we played in our jeans and runners and mismatched baseball caps. But, unexpectedly, we did develop team spirit, and rather than in-fighting, an us-against-them attitude prevailed.

We were so bad that there was no point taking ourselves seriously, like the other teams did. After a few games, my children were joined by some spouses and children and even some of the other renovators. They all applauded loudly if one of us actually hit or caught the ball and yelled encouragement when we did not. We usually had the biggest cheering section, even though we never actually won a game—although we did get two points when another team failed to show up for a game.

One of the members of our cheering section was Bob Adams, one of the renovators, whose wife had moved to her mother's home and had taken his three-year-old daughter with her. Bob was hesitant to approach any of the lawyers in our firm, as he felt he could not afford us. I only found out about his situation from Jason, who told me about it at one of our baseball games. I, in turn, spoke to John, who decided that because Bob was one of the louder members of our cheering section, we would take on his case on a pro bono basis.

Pro bono is short for the Latin phrase *pro bono public*, meaning "for the public good," and is work, usually legal representation, performed without compensation. Although many people see lawyers as money-hungry, almost all lawyers I know do some free legal work, often when children are involved. In Bob's case, his wife, who came from a very wealthy family, was refusing to let him see his daughter. Her family was paying her legal bills, and I suspect they thought he would simply give up because of his lack of funds. Imagine their surprise when John, one of the best-known family lawyers in town, filed a petition on his behalf.

While I was glad that John took Bob on pro bono, what it really meant was that I would be doing most of the work pro bono, which meant that the hours I worked on that file could not be billed. This in turn meant that I somehow had to find time to bill more hours. The only time was nights and weekends, meaning more time away from my children. Some weeks, the only time I saw them was late at night and at the firm's baseball games. I very seldom saw them in the morning, as by the time they got up, I was already long gone. Though the boys came to most of my baseball games, I made it to very few of theirs. I regret that.

I was usually able to find something humorous in the cases we took on. One that comes to mind is the husband who was ordered to leave his house but, prior to leaving, filled the curtain rods with raw shrimp. Talk about a smelly divorce! There was, however, nothing funny about Bob's situation.

Bob Adams's estranged wife was apparently willing to do anything to keep him out of their daughter's life. She alleged in her material that Bob had been sexually inappropriate with his daughter. This is bar none the worst allegation a person can make. Even if there is no truth to the claim, just making it affects the accused parent's life forever. No matter what happens, some people will always wonder if there is any truth to the accusation.

Mrs. Adams had taken their daughter to a child psychologist, who provided a report for the court. The psychologist had reached the conclusion that the little girl had been sexually abused because she exhibited certain behaviours, including changes in sleeping patterns, bed-wetting, nightmares and bad dreams, irritability and anger, and overaggressive behaviour for her young age. As the child was only three years old, the foregoing behaviours were described by the mother, not the child. They were the signs of possible sexual abuse, as described in books on the subject, which the mother quite likely looked up before visiting the psychologist. Furthermore, if the child was really exhibiting these behaviours, it could be because her mother had moved her to a new environment—one that did not include her dad.

Prior to a trial, in which the judge would make findings with respect to each party's credibility on an interim application, the judge gave our client only supervised visitation. With these kinds of allegations, the court will almost always take the position that it is better to err by protecting the child. As it would be almost a year before we could get a trial date, our client was only able to see his daughter with a supervisor present.

There are companies that provide supervisors, for a fee, and at the time, the fee was about 15 dollars per hour. The other option was to have a family member or close friend do the supervising.

Both choices have a downside. The paid supervisor can become quite expensive, plus it is difficult to have a visit with your child when a stranger is following you around. In some cases, the paid supervisor is required to provide a written report. It is problematic for the parent being supervised to be himself or herself knowing that there is going to be a "report card" on his or her behaviour.

Supervision by relatives or friends is obviously less expensive, but it can be complicated to find a person that both parties agree to. Bob's wife, Susan, suggested her mother or one of her sisters. For obvious reasons, Bob felt they would be too biased. Jason, the plumber who was working in our building, offered to supervise. Susan would not agree. After several suggestions from both parties, there was no agreement. Finally, Bob agreed to pay a supervisor, as, at this point, he had not seen his daughter for five weeks, which is a very long time for a three-year-old.

On top of paying for the supervisor, Bob was also paying child support of $375 per month. Accordingly, Bob could only afford to see his daughter four hours per week, which cost him $60 per week, or about $250 per month. Fortunately, Ruth and John decided that they wanted the washrooms in a totally different place in the building. This guaranteed at least four more months of steady work for Bob.

John had me hire a child psychologist to review the mother's psychologist's report and to observe John's interaction with his daughter during four of his supervised visits. In her report, our psychologist opined that the little girl was very comfortable and affectionate with her dad. She noted that on one occasion, the child ran into his arms at the beginning of the visit saying, "Daddy, I missed you." She wrote that Bob engaged the child in age-appropriate activities and included the supervisor as much as possible in an attempt to normalize the difficult situation.

When Bob's matter eventually came to trial, both of the child psychologists gave their opinion and were cross-examined by opposing counsel. Both Bob and his wife also gave evidence. Bob's wife, Susan, made unsubstantiated, exaggerated claims, as did her parents. They tried to paint a picture of an uninvolved father, who, they were sure, was inappropriate sexually with the child. There was no factual basis for their accusation; they simply "knew" that Bob should not spend any unsupervised time with his little girl.

Fortunately, the judge who heard the case was not interested in what Susan or her parents felt. He found that there was simply no evidence of inappropriate behaviour on Bob's part and was impressed that Bob had never missed a supervised visit in the 10 months prior to trial. In his Reasons for Judgement, the judge stated that he was tempted to give Bob sole custody in light of his wife's vicious, unsubstantiated allegations. Nonetheless, he felt that would not be in the child's best interest. He ordered that the parties have joint custody on a week on, week off basis.

The judge also ordered the wife to pay Bob's costs on the highest scale. That meant she had to pay costs as set out in the Rules of Court. Of course Bob had not incurred any legal fees but nonetheless was entitled, as it turned out, to $8,689 in costs. Bob wanted to give that money to John, but John generously declined. He had taken the case on pro bono and knew that Bob could really use the money.

Bob was another client with whom I kept in touch. The next summer, he came to our baseball games, with his daughter, if it was his week with her. After much coaxing, he agreed to play and was a fairly good player. On the nights he had his daughter, Sarah would watch her. He sent Christmas cards for many years, always enclosing a photograph of his little girl. Eventually, he remarried, and he and his new wife had a baby boy. We did, of course, see him for many months at our office working on the never-ending renovations.

After about 10 months of renovations, the office was in the same state of disarray as when I first came to work. The worst part was the drywall dust, which permeated all of my clothes and my hair. One of the offices being added was supposed to be for me; however, I was no closer to having a permanent place to work than I did when I started. To everyone's amusement, I finally bought one of those carts you see older ladies shopping with, so that I had some way of carting my work from one temporary "desk" to another.

Patrick was not amused by my cart or my general irreverence. Law was a serious enterprise for Patrick. He always looked impeccable. I never figured out how he stayed drywall-dust-free while the rest of us often looked like we had been caught in some sort of dust storm. I was leaving the office one night fairly late, and I noticed that Patrick was about to leave. I asked him if I could walk out to the parking lot with him, as we had heard that there was someone in the neighbourhood accosting women. Patrick agreed to walk out with me, but on the way to our cars, he said no one would attack someone my age. This lawyer apparently did not understand that rape has no discrimination. Women are at risk regardless of age, race, class, or what they look like.

As June came to an end so did the school year, and I began to worry about how I would occupy my children during the summer break. Sarah had been hired to work full-time at the Gap and was over the moon at the idea of having her own job and money. I did not want to rain on her parade by saying that she had to stay home with the boys but was at a loss as to how to keep them busy for the next two months. John came up with a solution. They could work with the renovators—sweeping, carrying supplies, picking up lunch, or whatever unskilled jobs were required. John claimed that he had cleared this plan with the builder ahead of time. I doubt very much that he asked them. It is more likely that he told them that the boys were going to be working with them.

Morgan and Mitchell were thrilled to have real jobs. I was concerned that it was simply a make-work project that had been forced on the renovation company. As it turned out, the boys worked harder than they ever had in their lives and came home most days exhausted, with no energy left to get into trouble. They went to work with me in the morning, but most days, they had to take the bus home at 5:00 p.m., as I was seldom finished with my work by then. The twins really grew up that summer. They had all sorts of male role models and never complained, no matter how menial the task.

They received paycheques from the contractor, but I was sure John was really paying all or some of their wages. They opened bank accounts and saved most of the money they earned, mainly because they were too tired to spend it.

John could be difficult to work for, but I will never forget how good he was to my boys (who were in awe and somewhat scared of him) and the compassion and generosity he showed to Bob Adams.

Chapter Eleven

July
Chang v. Chang

Mrs. Chang was referred to our firm by Mrs. Henderson, the woman who picketed her husband's veterinary clinic with a large sign stating he did not pay his child support. Sadly, Mrs. Chang's situation was not as easily solved.

Mr. Chang, who had a history of psychiatric illness, went to the corner store to buy some milk and bread and simply never returned. When Mrs. Chang came to our office, Mr. Chang had been gone for about five months. Apparently, he had gone missing on a number of occasions for a day or two and once for a week, so Mrs. Chang just kept hoping he would return. She had notified the police and checked regularly with all of the local hospitals but to no avail.

The parties had three children, who were nine, six, and three years old. Mrs. Chang had not worked outside the house since their first child was born. Mr. Chang had insisted that his wife stay home. Accordingly, she had been out of the workforce for close to 10 years. Mrs. and Mr. Chang were both accountants. His firm had continued to pay him for the past five months, but their largesse was coming to an end.

Until it can be established to a court's satisfaction that a person who has disappeared has died, all of the financial assets of that individual are frozen. To avoid a problem with Mr. Chang's paycheques, his firm had been depositing them to an account in Mrs. Chang's name. Other than that account, all of the parties' financial assets were in Mr. Chang's name and were frozen. Once the paycheques stopped, Mrs. Chang had absolutely no source of income.

Prior to coming to us, Mrs. Chang had sent out about 20 résumés, but no one had even given her an interview. She needed to take some courses and make herself more employable. Her hunt for a job reminded me of one of my interviews when I was looking for an articling position. I was interviewed by a young man who asked me if I planned to practise law or if I had just gone to law school out of interest.

I stood up, grabbed my purse, and, as I went to the door in what I hope was a haughty, dignified manner, said, "Yes, I studied 12 hours a day, seven days a week and ran up a large student loan simply because I was tired of bowling." I had 82 interviews before John hired me. I had good marks and lots of work and volunteer experience, but I was simply too old. John was the only lawyer who saw my age and my experience as a plus. For this too I will always be grateful.

The Changs owned considerable assets, including a mortgage-free house, RRSPs, investments, and two cars, both of which were new and had "all the bells and whistles." All of these assets were solely in Mr. Chang's name. Never having had a client with this particular problem, John sent me off to do some research, assuring Mrs. Chang that I would find a solution.

Mr. Chang had taken nothing with him, not even his wallet, presumably as he never intended to buy milk or bread. As far as Mrs. Chang could determine, he had no money, had not taken his passport, and had not used any of his credit cards. The only clothes that were missing were the ones he was wearing. All of these facts were important as evidence that Mr. Chang was probably dead.

According to my research, a person was presumed dead seven years after disappearing without explanation, unless other convincing evidence of his or her death can be found. The best evidence, of course, would be Mr. Chang's body, but although Mrs. Chang had been called by the police to view a number of unidentified bodies, none of them was her husband.

What Mrs. Chang needed was an order, pursuant to the Survivorship and Presumption of Death Act, presuming the death of her husband. To that end, I drafted Mrs. Chang's affidavit setting out why she thought he was dead: no money, no credit card charges, no passport, no contact with friends, no hospital admissions, and no contact with her, his parents, or his children. Mr. Chang was evidently a loving, involved father who, in Mrs. Chang's opinion, would not leave his children if he was still alive.

Because this was an unopposed application to the court, as an articling student, I could go to court on my own, but I was relieved when John decided to come with me. We were able to get into court very quickly, as there was no other party to serve. A short leave order was also not necessary, although I had wished I needed one, as I had become much better at them since my first disastrous day on the Peters case.

Much to my and Mrs. Chang's relief, the court found there was sufficient evidence to demonstrate that Mr. Chang had died. We were entitled to a presumption-of-death order. The next issue was what date Mr. Chang would be presumed to be dead. Some cases presumed the date of death as the last date the person was seen; others presumed the date of death as the date of the presumption-of-death order.

I argued successfully that Mr. Chang should be presumed dead on the last day he was seen, the date he went to buy milk and bread. He was presumed dead for all purposes as of that date, which meant that Mrs. Chang was entitled to Canada Pension Plan benefits and life insurance benefits backdated to the date he disappeared. All of their financial assets were unfrozen (or, as I pictured them, thawed out).

Because I had done most of the work on this file, John let me do most of the talking. It was classified as a final order, which meant that we had to wear our trial attire, including gowns, shirt tabs, and vests. As we were walking toward the courthouse, John realized that he had forgotten his notes. He sent me back to get them, and he and Mrs. Chang proceeded to the courthouse.

When I got to the courtroom, John was introducing himself to the judge, in my gown. I am five feet one inch, and he is about six-four. How he put on my robe without noticing I'll never know. I had no choice but to put on his robe before I entered the courtroom. Fortunately, the judge had a sense of humour and called a short recess so we could trade robes. While I would have been mortified, John saw his mistake as funny and simply carried on with his part of the submissions.

Mr. Chang had a will in which he left everything to his wife. This meant the house could be transferred to her, as could all of his RRSPs and investments. Mrs. Chang received $150,000 from her husband's life insurance, most of which she put away for her children's education. The balance of the funds she planned to use to upgrade her education and to pay her legal bill, which was fairly substantial. As most of the time on the file was mine, Mr. Chang's disappearance helped to increase my billable hours for July. Part of me felt guilty about gaining from someone else's loss and unhappiness, but I must admit I mostly felt relieved that my hours had increased significantly.

As far as I know, Mr. Chang was never found. Although Mrs. Chang felt bad about her children losing their father, I believe she was also relieved that she no longer had to deal with a mentally ill husband, who, she told me after everything was finalized, had been both mentally and physically abusive to her throughout their marriage.

Clearly Mrs. Chang had mixed emotions with respect to her late husband. Losing him in the way she did was a shock, but

I believe she was also relieved. She had been unable to leave what had been an abusive relationship on her own accord. His disappearance had made the decision for her.

Over the years, I saw a number of women and one man who had stayed in abusive marriages for years, hoping their spouses would change, as they promised. I met with clients who had been seriously beaten, sustaining black eyes, cigarette burns, and broken bones. Some had been mentally and verbally abused to the extent that they had no sense of self-worth. It is difficult for those of us who have not experienced abuse to understand why people stay in these relationships. However, battered woman (or men) syndrome is a recognized psychological condition, which has been generally broken down into four stages by various experts in the field. Their findings can be summarized as follows:

Stage One—Denial

- Women deny to others that they have a problem.
- They make excuses for any abusive incident.
- They believe that the abuse will never again be repeated.

Stage Two—Guilt

- Women acknowledge that there is a problem.
- They begin to question their own character and try to live up to their partner's expectations.

Stage Three—Enlightenment

- Women begin to understand that they do not deserve to be beaten up.

- They stay in an attempt to keep the relationship intact, hoping that their partner will change.

Stage Four—Responsibility

- Women realize that their partner has a problem that only he can fix.
- They come to understand that there is nothing they can do to change their partner.
- They may take the necessary steps to leave and begin a new life.

Women who are physically and mentally abused over an extended period of time may show signs of fearfulness and hopelessness, but still, in many cases, they do not leave. This may be because they are afraid that the abuse will escalate and may even become fatal if they try to leave. Some women lack the support of family and friends and fear that, as a single parent, they will face financial hardship. Some may not know where to get help and rationalize that there still are some good times.

Most abuse cases are men abusing women, but I did have one case where a husband was being abused by his wife. When Mr. Johnson came to our office, he was clearly afraid of his wife. He brought photographs of his various injuries, including one in which he had two black eyes and another in which his wife had knocked out two of his front teeth. He also brought a picture of his wife, who was clearly much bigger than he. Although John advised Mr. Johnson that he should get out of the house before the abuse got worse, he was not very sympathetic to Mr. Johnson's plight. Accordingly, Mr. Johnson became my client.

He was afraid of his wife but was reluctant to leave, as he was worried that if his wife did not have him as a punching bag, she would turn on his children, who were five and seven years old. We decided to bring a court application for interim custody. I did advise him that it may be difficult to get full custody, but we could hope a judge would make an order giving them equal time with the children.

As it was Mr. Johnson's application, I gave my submissions first. I had only been speaking for about two or three minutes when I heard an uproar behind me. When I turned around, Mrs. Johnson was coming toward me with a knife in her hand. Fortunately, there was a sheriff in the courtroom. It took him and three lawyers, who were waiting their turn, to keep her away from me. As they forcibly removed her from the courtroom, she called me every name you could think of—most of which I am reluctant to relate.

This was one scary lady. She weighed about 300 pounds and appeared to be incredibly strong. Needless to say, Mr. Johnson was awarded interim custody of the children and sole interim possession of the family home. Mrs. Johnson was charged with attempted assault and was ordered to complete an anger-management course.

Mr. Johnson was incredibly grateful for our "win," which, in reality, had very little to do with me but mostly to do with his wife's behaviour. I do not think that Mr. Johnson had ever before come out on the winning side since he married his wife. Of course, the battle was not won, as I was sure Mrs. Johnson would not just go away. I suggested that while Mrs. Johnson was taking her anger-management course, Mr. Johnson should take some assertiveness training.

I read somewhere that abuse is one of the top 10 reasons for divorce, ranking number six after money, cheating, addictions, lack of communication, and growing apart. I have read a lot about battered wife (and husband) syndrome, and why people stay in abusive marriages for years, but I still find it hard to understand. As someone who is not fond of pain, I believe I would be out of there after the first black eye, broken nose, etc., but it is hard to say if you have never been in that situation.

My former husband had never been abusive to me or our children. He simply was not present most of the time, even when we lived together. He lived his own life, as if he did not have a family. Growing up as an only child, he never had chores, nor did he ever have a part-time job when he was at school. I suspect that his stay-at-home mother followed him around cleaning up after him. After he had a shower, he would drop the towel wherever he happened to be. Similarly, his dirty clothes remained wherever he stepped out of them. If he made himself toast, the butter, jam, and bread were left on the counter. He never put a dish in the sink or the dishwasher.

I was determined that my sons would learn to clean up after themselves, so that I did not bring up replicas of their father. It helped that their father did not live with us so they would not grow up thinking some woman would pick up after them. I also think that there were some advantages to my long hours. My children had to learn to be self-sufficient. This theory, if nothing else, helped me deal with the guilt I felt because of my time spent at work.

Our softball league ended at the end of July. It had been fun, but it did involve two nights a week when I was not home until about 10:00 p.m. However, it had become a family outing, as most nights, the boys came to watch us lose. It was a source of amusement to them. Often, they collapsed into peals of laughter on the way home as they relived our incompetence.

Chapter Twelve

August
Called to the Bar

August was my last month of articling; I would then be called to the bar. This is a ceremony in which the students who have passed the bar exams and completed their articling year are officially called to the bar, meaning they can practice law in British Columbia. Dressed in full court attire, one by one, the students are called to the stage, given certificates, and welcomed to the practice of law by a panel of judges.

It is a rather solemn occasion, and everyone usually claps politely after each name is called; however, when my name was called, my children, who had taken part and helped me on the journey that had culminated in this day, shouted, "Way to go, Mom!" Although some parents and students looked aghast, as he handed me my certificate, the Honourable Chief Justice said, "This lady is very lucky to have children who are so proud of her."

More important, I was extremely proud of them. They had put up with my long hours with minimal complaint and, especially Sarah, had helped with the running of the house. Getting me to be a "real lawyer" had been a family effort and had involved sacrifices on my children's parts.

The next step for me was to get a job. I had asked John on a number of occasions if he would keep me on as a full-fledged lawyer. His answer was always, "We will have to see when the time comes." Well, the time was fast approaching. At the end of August, my articling year would be over and I would be unemployed. On about August 15 I asked John once again, and he said, "Of course you have a job here," as if it had been a foregone conclusion.

I suspect I asked him at just the right time, as he had a six-week trial coming up and he needed my help. I had done most of the preparation for the trial, including putting documents and case law books together. I had interviewed the client numerous times and even flown to his house on one of the gulf islands to sort documents. It was the first time I had been in a small floatplane, and I was quite surprised when the pilot jumped out of the plane and tied it up at the dock. Because my family had always had motorboats, I knew the drill and jumped out of the plane to tie up the back rope. Apparently, I was the only passenger who had ever done this. The astonished pilot thanked me and then diplomatically advised that, because of liability issues, passengers were not expected to help with the mooring.

Our client met me at the dock and took me for a tour of the island before we went to his house, which was amazing. It was about 6,000 square feet with an indoor/outdoor pool and a nine-hole golf course. After his wife left him, our client had lived alone in the house, except for a full-time housekeeper. I soon learned that he was a neat freak when he made me a sandwich for lunch and then instructed me to eat it over the sink. I felt about nine years old as he stood and watched me to ensure I did not drop any crumbs on his immaculate floor.

As well as having to eat over the sink, shoes were not allowed in the house and cushions were plumped the minute you got up, either by him or his ever-present housekeeper. Dishes were washed by hand rather than in the top-of-the-line dishwasher, as it saved on electricity. I was advised that I could have a shower, but it should be no longer than three minutes. I did have a very fast shower, all the while picturing him lurking outside the door with a stopwatch. The room in which I had to sort through documents was not heated, as only the few rooms he actually used were heated—and they were kept just above freezing.

Although it was August, I was working in the cold basement and spent most of two days with a coat, hat, and gloves on. I wondered if his cheapness and excessive neatness had helped to drive his wife away. It certainly made me work as fast as I could so I could get back to my messy, warm house. Unfortunately, this man's neatness did not extend to his documents. There was no filing system or common sense to the piles of paper I had to review. For instance the statements for his several bank accounts were all in a box, mixed together in no particular order.

Besides being a cheap neat freak, our client was quite deaf. Accordingly, as well as being cold, by the time I left, I was hoarse from yelling my questions to him. In addition, he never left me alone in the basement. He said he would "keep me company," but I suspect he just wanted someone to talk to, someone to listen to his complaints about his wife. So the whole time I was trying to make sense of his documents, I had to carry on a very loud conversation with him. As well as a litany of complaints about his estranged wife, my client "entertained" me by relating an interminable list of really bad lawyer jokes. I assume he had looked them up in a book as it was before the advent of the Internet. Most of his jokes were about greed, excess billing, and stupid questions asked in court; some of which were as follows:

Question: What do you call 500 dead lawyers at the bottom of the ocean?

Answer: A good start

Question: Why don't sharks attack lawyers?

Answer: Professional courtesy

Question: What is the difference between a lawyer and a herd of buffalo?

Answer: A lawyer charges more.

Question: How many lawyers does it take to screw in a light bulb?

Answer: One—the lawyer holds the light bulb and the rest of the world revolves around him.

Question: How can you tell when a lawyer is lying?

Answer: His lips are moving.

Question: What is the problem with lawyer jokes?

Answer: Lawyers do not think they are funny, and no one else thinks they are jokes.

Some of the "stupid questions" asked in court included the following:

Question: She has three children?

Answer: Yes.

Question: How many are boys?

Answer: None.

Question: Were there any girls?

Question: I am showing you exhibit three. Do you recognize that photo?

Answer: It is me.

Question: Were you present when the photo was taken?

Question: Your first marriage was terminated by death?

Answer: Yes.

Question: By whose death was it terminated?

And my personal favourite:

Question: Have you lived in this town all of your life?

Answer: Not yet.

All of us have asked a stupid question at one time or another, especially when we are first starting out. A courtroom can be an intimidating place, especially if you draw a difficult judge. My first few times I went to court, I included my name in my notes as well as whom I was acting for, just in case I went totally blank. But all my carefully prepared notes were of little use to me in my very first trial when I accidentally knocked over my glass of water with the sleeve of my gown. Because soggy notes are hard to read, after the court clerk mopped up the water, I was forced to "wing it."

As a gift to commemorate my call to the bar, my former husband gave me an ornately framed copy of Shakespeare's quote from *Henry VI* (Part 2): "The first thing we do let's kill all the lawyers." The play revolves around the War of the Roses (1455–1485) and was first printed in about 1597. What my former husband and many others don't know is that Shakespeare did not mean this line as a cut or a dig against lawyers, but a dig against commercial life and government. It is agreed by Shakespeare scholars that the point of the play is that the surest way to chaos and tyranny is to remove the lawyers, the guardians of independent thinking. Today, people use this quote out of context, but to Shakespeare, it was an attempt to underscore the important role that lawyers play in society. I tried to explain the real meaning to my ex-husband, but he was not interested. He wanted to believe that he had insulted my new profession. I think he was quite surprised when I hung the nicely framed quote in a prominent place in my kitchen, where I see it every day and enjoy the irony of his gift.

Although I have, over the years, dealt with a few obnoxious lawyers, they have been few and far between. Like in any profession, there are a few bad apples, but generally, I have found my colleagues to be trustworthy and pleasant. Most do some pro bono work, and many take on legal-aid cases, which pay next to nothing. The majority of lawyers attempt to settle cases rather than put their clients through the financial and emotional cost of a trial.

Most of my cases that did end up in a trial did so because the clients refused to compromise. Some want to tell their side of the story even though, aside from the court clerk and the judge, who have heard it all before, their only audience usually is the other party and the lawyers. Sadly, I have seen a number of cases where the parties paid most of their money to lawyers rather than meet each other halfway.

In addition to the Shakespeare quotation, I also received a framed copy of the well-known exchange between Lady Aster and Winston Churchill:

Lady Aster: "If you were my husband, I would poison your tea."

Winston Churchill: "If you were my wife, I would drink it."

My sister thought this was an appropriate gift for someone who was crazy enough to practice family law. This gift hangs in my kitchen next to the Shakespeare quote. Just looking at them helps me to see the humour in many of my cases—humour that is not evident to my stressed-out clients.

My children, with the help of my parents, gave me a much more practical gift—a new sewing machine. I assume they were letting me know that I might be a lawyer, but I still had to do the mending. In all fairness, it was a thoughtful and very much appreciated gift. I enjoy sewing but had struggled with, and sworn at, an antiquated machine for years. My new one ran like a charm and did all sorts of fancy stitches and even buttonholes. It also had a zipper foot.

When I returned from my trip to the island with the documents I felt were relevant, it took me a while to quit speaking to my children and my colleagues in the loud voice I had had to use with our client. John talked back to me in a very loud voice and acted as if I had had a little holiday, rather than a very stressful two days with "Mr. Neatness." He immediately gave me a file I had never seen before. It was Friday, and he needed a written argument for the Court of Appeal for Monday. Friday night when I got home, I really appreciated my usually messy, noisy, warm house where nobody had to eat their lunch hanging over the sink, although when I told Sarah about the sink episode, she suggested it would be a good idea to have the twins eat this way.

My children seemed happy to see me—not so much, I suspect, because they missed me but because they were glad to see my parents leave. My mom and dad had kindly offered to watch my children when I was away; however, they were much stricter than I was and ran the house as they had their house when I was a child. My dad was in the military his whole working life, and our house was like a military base. The good news for me was that when I arrived home, my house was spotless, and, as my mom advised when they left, everything was shipshape.

Although I knew it would not stay that way for long, it was satisfying to come home to a house that was shipshape, as I had to do a quick turn-around and go back to the office Saturday morning. I just had time to listen to my children's complaints about my parents and commiserate. There were none of their usual grievances about each other, as they had a common enemy. Just to be clear, my mom and dad loved my children; they just had a different way of running a house. Apparently, my dad had everyone up and reporting for duty by 8:00 a.m. Over breakfast, he assigned the chores for the day. My children admitted, however, that the two days were not all bad.

The first night, my parents took them to a movie. Being cognisant of how embarrassing it would be for the children to be seen with their grandparents, my parents diplomatically sat two rows behind them. On Sunday, the "drill master" dropped them off at the mall once their chores were done and gave them each 50 dollars to spend as they saw fit. Sarah bought herself two very nice outfits, and the twins spent their money on a couple of rude T-shirts, which they had the good sense not to show my parents, and so much junk food they were unable to eat the roast beef dinner my mother had lovingly prepared for my return.

Saturday morning I was back in the office reading the file John had given me on Friday afternoon. An argument for the Court of Appeal is a written argument called a factum. It must be prepared in a certain fashion, stating the issue or issues on appeal and why you believe the Supreme Court judge's ruling was wrong, either on the facts or in law. This involves referring to the relevant documents, which were presented at the trial, and to the transcript of the trial. You then cite any case law that supports your position.

Prior to drafting the factum, I had five days of transcripts to read, looking for evidence and errors that would substantiate our arguments. Reading the transcripts and researching the case law took most of Saturday. By five o'clock, my brain had stopped working. I phoned home and let my children know I would be home in about half an hour with yet another pizza. I also called Caroline and arranged for her to come to the office at 12:00 p.m. on Sunday so she could start typing the part of the factum I would have dictated by then.

I started dictating about 9:00 a.m. Sunday morning. At approximately 11:30 a.m., much to my horror, the tape I was using broke. All my careful dictation, including case cites and citation of the appropriate exhibit numbers and transcript pages and line numbers, was unravelling before my eyes. I felt myself falling apart. I had more or less kept it together throughout an incredibly stressful year—a year that, in addition to unreasonable, demanding clients, included

- dealing with John's ever-changing moods and often indecipherable instructions;
- begging Jazmin for a new pencil, dictation tapes, or paper and the use of "her" fax machine;
- avoiding Ruth, who had wasted hours of my time;
- untangling Jacquelynn's bookkeeping blunders;
- writing a chapter on child support for the new *Family Law Manual*, a time-consuming exercise, which John had volunteered to write;

- finding an empty office or a pile of wood where I could work;
- hunting for files, which were kept in no particular order; and
- organizing the Christmas party and delivering turkeys.

None of the foregoing counted as hours that I could bill, so meeting my quota of billable hours meant working late and many weekends. In addition to the work-related stress, there were the home-related stressors, such as the trip to emergency after Morgan set Mitchell's Halloween costume on fire with a sparkler; the emergency doctor was not impressed, no doubt because our family were regular visitors to emergency.

In December, Mitchell decided to climb up on the roof so he could hang the Christmas lights. Our old ladder collapsed, and he fell on his foot. Because he could walk on it, I decided it wasn't broken and told him to put a cold cloth on it, my remedy for most of their mishaps. The next morning, his ankle was twice its normal size, so I took him to emergency. The same doctor was on duty; he was not at all pleased that I had waited almost 48 hours to bring my son with a broken ankle to the hospital.

Then there was the time my temporary cap fell off my front tooth and down the bathroom sink on a day I was going to court. Thankfully, my next-door neighbour came over with a wrench and retrieved the cap. I was so afraid that it would fall off in court that I affixed it in place with crazy glue. My dentist was not happy, but apparently, the twins' class was, as my boys thought it was a funny story to relate at show-and-tell.

There was the also the day I went to the Surrey courthouse only to find that it was no longer there. I eventually found the new one an hour and a half later than I was expected. The judge was not impressed.

We had no heat in our house for November and most of December, as I did not have enough money to feed us and fill the empty oil tank. When my parents dropped in a couple of days before Christmas and saw us wearing winter coats, gloves, scarves, and hats in the house, they were not happy. The tank of oil they gave us for Christmas was one of best gifts we had ever received.

The broken dictation tape was the proverbial straw that broke me. My research indicates that the idiom, "the straw that broke the camel's back" is from an Arabic proverb about how a camel is loaded beyond its capacity to move or stand. It describes the one last thing that finally makes you upset and can break you and causes you to fall apart. There is a limit to everyone's endurance, and apparently, this was my breaking point.

When Caroline arrived at the office, I was sobbing so loud that it took me some time to explain the problem. Caroline gave me a long, hard hug. Then she handed me a glass of water and a box of Kleenex and told me that she knew a guy who could repair the tape. Caroline always had "a guy" who could acquire, find, and fix things. The "tape guy" arrived at our office within the hour and fixed the tape in about10 minutes. He seemed to be in a hurry to fix the problem and leave. I suspect his rush was to get away from the crazy lady huddled in the corner thanking him profusely in between hiccoughing sobs.

Once again, Caroline had come to my rescue. In about three more hours, I had finished my dictation, with Caroline typing it up as I went. While I was dictating, Caroline had also done up cover pages, indexes, and the bibliography. By approximately 4:30 p.m., we had retired to the bar next door for a celebratory drink.

The next Friday, in the rotunda of the courthouse, was the ceremony where about 30 of us were called to the bar. My children and parents were there, as was Caroline. The ceremony was over by about 1:00 p.m., and we went out to lunch, and then I went home rather than going back to the office. I took Friday afternoon and the whole weekend off. I felt I had earned two and a half days off. I had had my mini-breakdown but had made it to the finish line without completely losing my sense of balance.

CPSIA information can be obtained at www.ICGtesting.com
Printed in the USA
LVOW041704160712

290293LV00004B/157/P